Sanguine Bastille

J.R. Shepherd

Sanguine Bastille

Contents

Epilogue 187

Academy Primer

The World of The Academy

On Sorcerers

In the world of The Academy, many people are born with the ability to use magic. These people, called sorcerers, can use the force of their own will to manipulate the natural energy that flows through the world to temporarily change the world around them.

The Academy is a school that operates throughout the entire world to teach sorcerers how to control their power so that it won't cause harm to others or the world around them.

To give each sorcerer an education that matches their own skills and strengths, each sorcerer goes through a ceremony and draws three cards from a special deck of playing cards.

The number on the cards they draw, starting from Two and going up to Ace, show how naturally strong a sorcerer is in each of the types of magic they can use. The average for most sorcerers fall between Four and Six.

The Royal cards, Jacks, Queens, and Kings, are as powerful as Aces. However, their strength comes with a destiny in store for them. A destiny to rule, or lead, and walk side by side with other Royal Suits.

The Suit of each card a sorcerer draws shows what type of magic they personally resonate with the most and can often also reflect the personality of the individual in many ways.

-Spades are quick, aggressive casters. Seen as warriors and defenders who resonate with destructive magic and are skilled at using magic without speaking spells out loud. Their internal reservoir of power is small but recovers quickly when used up.

-Hearts are powerful spellcasters who become even stronger when working alongside others. They are capable of casting many kinds of magic, but often resonate with magics of a particular natural element. They have enormous internal reservoirs of strength but, if it runs dry, it can take a long time to recover completely.

-Clubs are very closely attuned to the spiritual and natural worlds. They can sense spirits and communicate with them. They can also become very skillful healers and excel at casting magic with spoken incantations to focus their power. Their internal reservoirs are limited but not as much as Spades.

-Diamonds are a special suit. They are very sensitive to the world and can feel even the slightest thing out of place. They excel at extremely simple magic, called cantrips, but begin to fail when trying to cast higher levels of magic. Despite this handicap to their spellcasting, they are excellent at joining others in casting magic as a group. Diamonds are also capable of catching glimpses of the future. Lower level Diamonds can sense something might happen, or suddenly feel they know something they shouldn't. However, the higher level Diamonds can often learn to see specific details of the future at will.

On Aspects

Aspects are humans who have inherited animal blood, be that through their bloodline or the blessing of an animal spirit. The Aspects gain senses and abilities from their animal blood that allow them to do things others cannot. Most Aspects do very little beyond enhancing certain senses, but there are a few who gain special abilities.

The most powerful Aspects, by far, are those rare few individuals who receive an Aspect from one of the twelve Zodiac signs. These individuals gain great strengths, depending on the person and which sign they gained. However, only around one to two percent of all aspects are Zodiac Aspects.

On Curse-Bloods

Curse-Bloods are humans who's ancestors encountered a dark secret and were cursed from it. The curse always passed to their children and was quickly fatal. So, the three elders of the Curse-Bloods each sought out a way to keep their children safe from the curse running in their blood. They found two answers.

The first two elders called upon the King and Queen of The Fey for protection. The Fey agreed and a pact was forged. The humans who became protected under this pact became Vampires. So long as the Vampires adhere to the rules of the Pact, their lives will be long and their children protected under the same pact the moment their Cursed Blood awakens.

The third elder made an agreement with a great Wolf Spirit from The Fey Wilds. Those humans protected by this agreement became Werewolves. Their lives are normal and unburdened by the Cursed Blood, but in return they must take wolf form and join the Wolf Spirit when he hunts. This happens during each full moon, and during the Wild Hunt of The Fey Wilds.

Both types of Curse-Bloods, Vampires and Werewolves, are separated into three castes based on the strength of their Cursed Blood.

The first caste of Curse-Bloods, making up roughly sixty percent of all Curse-Bloods, are Drone-class for Vampires, and Waifs for Werewolves.

Waifs, once they have transformed under the full moon, cannot control themselves and will seek out prey, or follow the lead of another nearby Werewolf of a higher caste.

Drones have all the strengths and long life of other Vampires, but they are trapped in a cycle of a short waking day and long days of rest. Each Drone wakes for twenty-four hours and, once that time has passed, they collapse and sleep for six days. These

Drones are separated into groups, called Suites, that are organized based on what day of the week they are awake.

The second caste of Curse-Bloods, making up thirty to thirty-five percent of all Curse-Bloods, are Lord-class for Vampires, and Alphas for Werewolves.

Alphas are larger than Waifs and, when they transform under a full moon, cannot fight their need to hunt but retain much of their normal human intelligence. This makes them far more dangerous as they can plan out attacks, rather than simply chasing prey, and can lead groups of waifs to trap prey that might otherwise escape. A hunting pack of Werewolves rarely grows larger than four or five individuals.

Lord-class Vampires have the same strength and long life as the Drones do, but are not limited to a long sleep schedule. They sleep on the same kind of schedule that any normal human does, though they risk collapsing if they try to stay up much longer than twenty-four hours. Lord-class Vampires also awaken special powers that allow them to manipulate a single one of the four elements.

The third caste of Curse-Bloods, making up only five to ten percent of all Curse-Bloods, are Archlord-class for Vampires, and Archons for Werewolves.

Archons are even larger than Alphas and have full control over their transformations and also their mind and senses when transformed. They are able to resist the urge to hunt and are, therefore, able to avoid harming innocent people during the full moon.

Archlord-class Vampires have all the strengths and abilities of the Lord-class vampires. They can stay awake for longer, though they still run the risk of collapse if they stay awake for too long. Archlord-class Vampire also have the ability to 'Command' vampires who are of lesser castes, or who are weaker minded than themselves, and force them to do as they command.

Prologue

Hivelord Andros checked his watch.

"I suppose it is about time for the moon to rise. Are we fully prepared?" He asked, pushing a lock of silver hair away from his clean-shaven face.

Overlord Burchard, a much older-looking man, leaned forward and tapped on the glass tabletop, refreshing the embedded screens.

"It appears so, Hivelord. The other America-based Hives have sent Lord class Vampires to patrol every major city in the U.S. and the Werewolf Enclaves are ensuring, to the best of their ability, that all but the Archon class Werewolves are under lock and key."

Hivelord Andros nodded and turned to the third man at the table.

"What about you, Alaric? Are the enforcers reporting anything amiss?"

Underlord Alaric, a seemingly young man with long silver hair, glanced back and forth between the table screens and a tablet he held in his right hand.

"Most are reporting all clear, and the rest are reporting low risk. Headmaster Daedalus on the east coast and Headmaster Orpheus on the west coast both state that The Academy is ready to give aid in the event of an emergency."

The Hivelord nodded.

"Very good, though I hope there will be no need for the sorcerers to interfere."

Underlord Alaric nodded his agreement.

Overlord Burchard grumbled, staring down at the screens, trying to pick out one group among thousands.

"Where are our own enforcers currently? We should not let them stray too far from us. We must ensure that the Quintessence mines remain secure."

Underlord Alaric tapped his tablet a few times and then swiped across it, a windowed view sliding from the tablet onto the table screens.

"They left Fort Worth an hour ago heading north. They will make multiple stops, leaving Lord-class vampires in each area populated by more than eighteen hundred people as they head towards Oklahoma City. Around the time the moon is setting, Suite Lord Angelica will make her way west until an hour before dawn, at which time she will call all our people to return to the Hive."

Overlord Burchard grumbled again.

"Are they not straying too far from us?"

Hivelord Andros chuckled.

"All will be well, Burchard. We are here, along with most of the Suite Lords and the two hundred and thirty-six Drone class vampires that are currently awake. There are few who could successfully attack a Hive of that strength, let alone one as well protected as ours. Besides, I doubt even Alaric would be able to coax Angelica back before daybreak."

The Underlord chuckled.

"Angie wants to make sure the full moon passes without casualty on any side. Unless an emergency occurs, I doubt she will listen to anyone."

Overlord Burchard huffed.

"You should keep your Blood-bonded on a shorter leash."

"And you should keep your tongue on an even shorter one." Underlord Alaric smiled politely, but his eyes flashed dangerously.

Hivelord Andros held up his hand.

"That's enough, both of you. Don't provoke Alaric, Burchard. You should know better. I already approved this course of action weeks ago. As the Great Plains Hive, we have a responsibility to ensure that those of Cursed Blood are protected and prevented from harming the Pure Blood populace. During the last full moon a handful of werewolves slipped through our nets and people died because of it. The Elders want to ensure we do not allow such a thing to happen again."

Overlord Burchard clasped his hands together, looking down at them but saying nothing.

"Angelica is our strongest enforcer, but she is by no means our only defense. Our first line of defense is keeping the location of this Hive secret. Keeping many Lords around us at this time would only compromise our ability to remain hidden."

The Hivelord sighed.

"Now, let us set this matter aside. We must ensure this night goes by without incident. We may discuss how best to handle future full moons at a later date."

Both men nodded to the Hivelord, who tapped on the table to change to a map of the entire United States.

"Good. Then start in the south and move upwards and out. Ensure each team reports in and has every bit of support they need. We will carry the world on our shoulders, through until the morning."

1

Chapter One

Liam groaned, lifting his head off of his computer desk and blinking the sleep from his eyes. After several long moments, he realized the office was dark and a few seconds of looking around started to fill his chest with a sense of dread.

"Did I... fall asleep?" He muttered to himself, trying to breathe deeply to slow his rapidly increasing heart rate.

He quickly stood up, knocking over the empty mug on his desk, and rushed over to the window that looked out onto the street.

He looked upwards and his heart sank as he saw that the full moon was already starting to dip low in the sky.

"Shoot. Of all days to fall asleep at work, I had to choose the full moon."

He stepped backward and stumbled over a garbage can, barely catching himself on the edge of another desk. He righted himself and rubbed his aching chest, turning towards the back of the office.

"Ok, Liam, try to calm down. There probably wouldn't be any werewolves on this end of town anyway."

He flinched as he accidentally knocked over a desk fan with his elbow and fumbled to turn it back upright.

"It's only one block from the back door of the office to the apartment. It won't be that bad. Just a quick walk."

He struggled through the dark office, tripping on a few boxes that had been stacked near the back door, and paused as his hand landed on the door handle.

"It's fine. There aren't any werewolves out tonight. It's just a quick walk. No one will even realize you were such an idiot."

He tried to force his heart to slow down, then carefully opened the door and peeked outside.

The alley behind the office was quiet and still. Taking comfort in this, Liam stepped out and quietly closed the door behind him.

Immediately he thought he had heard a low growl nearby and quickly tried to turn and go back into the office, but the office door had clicked shut and wouldn't open from the outside.

Liam looked around in a panic and quickly rushed across the alley. He pressed himself into the doorway of an old shop, trying to hide himself in the shadows cast by the, now setting, full moon.

He could now clearly hear a werewolf somewhere nearby, growling and sniffing at the air. He peaked out around the corner towards the main street, trying to see if he could catch a glimpse of where the werewolf was before slipping away.

The alley was mostly empty, populated by a few small garbage cans and bits of trash. After a few minutes, he could no longer hear the werewolf and hoped that meant it had moved on. He carefully turned the other direction and stepped out of the doorway.

He was immediately struck by a hot, foul-smelling breath and he found himself staring directly into a pair of piercing yellow eyes.

The werewolf's lips curled in a sneer, revealing shockingly white teeth in perfect rows.

Liam stood perfectly still, his heart pounding heavily in his chest, hoping that somehow the werewolf would forget about him and leave.

The werewolf's teeth began to open, another wave of foul breath escaping its mouth, and it reached out with its clawed, almost human-like, hands.

Liam braced himself to turn and sprint as fast as he could but, as he started to twist his feet to push away, a high-pitched whistle pierced the air.

The werewolf flinched and a flash of flame above them lit the alley. A woman with long and wavy bright red hair dropped from the rooftop above them and twisted in the air to strike the werewolf in the head with a powerful ax kick. The werewolf struck the ground with a yelp and half rolled onto its side before going still.

The woman stood up straight, shaking her head and brushing some hair out of her face. She was wearing a black gothic coat with red trim, which she tugged on to straighten.

"You do realize it's a bad idea to go outside during a full moon, right?" She asked.

Liam blinked in surprise, slowly processing what had just happened.

"I'm sorry. I was... I mean, thank you for helping me... I fell asleep at work... I mean, I lost track of time..." Liam realized he was rambling, eyes unwillingly drawn to the werewolf at their feet.

The woman frowned at him, inspecting him with her bright green eyes.

"You really should get off the streets. Do you live near here at least?"

Liam nodded nervously.

"Yes, I'm sorry. I only live a block over from where I work. I thought I could get back before I was noticed by anything."

The woman sighed, nudging the werewolf with her foot to make sure it was unconscious.

"Alright then, let's go. I'll escort you."

Liam jerked slightly in surprise.

"Relax kid, I won't bite."

The woman smirked, revealing a clean white smile. Though it was clear she was trying to hide her long, sharp canine teeth.

Liam nodded, keeping his eyes pointed at the ground.

"Sorry, I'm a bit on edge."

"As you should be." The woman paused, her nostrils flaring as she smelled the air.

"Get back!" She yelled, pushing Liam away.

Liam stumbled back and fell, landing on his back with a grunt. As he landed, he saw another, larger werewolf pounce from the dark onto the woman. Its mouth clamped down on her left shoulder, sinking its long teeth into her.

The woman growled in pain but remained on her feet.

"Get out of here kid, I'll deal with this one. Run!"

As she spoke, the woman reached over with her right hand and grabbed the werewolf by the back of its neck. With a grunt, she lifted it off the ground and spun, slamming it into the nearby brick buildings.

Liam scrambled backward, twisting to get onto his feet, and took off out of the alley and onto the sidewalk near the street. He slid around the corner, doing his best to stay on his feet, and ran along the sidewalk as fast as he could towards the street that would take him around to the other end of the alley he had been in before.

Almost by instinct he dropped to the ground and slid past the corner, off the sidewalk, and into the street.

Another werewolf pounced at Liam from around the buildings but slammed into the traffic light as Liam slid by and flipped around in the air, landing on its back with a snarl.

Without looking back, Liam jumped back up onto his feet and sprinted full speed down the middle of the road. He could hear the werewolf growling behind him, scrambling back onto its feet, and he pushed himself to go faster.

He made a wide turn around the final corner and headed towards his apartment building. A crash behind Liam told him the werewolf hadn't taken the corner as wide, and had slid into a pair of newspaper stands.

Liam ran almost full speed into the door to his apartment complex and grasped the handle, yanking the door with all his strength. His heart sank when the door refused to budge and he realized it had been locked for the night.

He slowly turned around and watched the werewolf walking towards him, on all fours, with a look that amounted to amusement.

Liam braced himself, clenching his teeth and leaning against the door, certain that he was about to become a particularly lean meal for this werewolf.

"You know, kid, you're pretty quick on your feet."

Liam felt himself take a sharp breath as the woman from before gently drifted down to the ground in front of him, her red hair glowing like flames and floating weightlessly around her.

"I can't say I know many Pure-Bloods who could outrun a werewolf on the hunt."

The werewolf in the street had stopped and was now baring its teeth at the woman, growling softly.

The woman growled back.

"Ungrateful Waif. If I wasn't here to stop you, the Enclave would have you executed for killing another human being. You should appreciate me more."

She took a step forward and, in a fraction of a second, she closed the distance between her and the werewolf. Without a moment's hesitation, she raised her fist and struck the werewolf over the head, a fiery explosion knocking it to the ground.

The werewolf yelped and tried to roll back onto its feet again. The woman planted a kick into its side, knocking it into the air. She twisted with a graceful pirouette, lifting her leg above her head and bringing her foot down hard, slamming the werewolf back into the ground with a burst of flame.

The werewolf struck the ground, with enough force to crack the asphalt and send a shudder down the street, grunted once, then collapsed into a motionless heap.

The woman shook her head and ran her fingers through her hair as the fiery glow faded away. She sighed and turned back to Liam.

"Are you alright over there, kid? You're not hurt, are you?"

Liam quickly nodded, then changed his mind and tried to shake his head and speak, though he wasn't able to force out any sounds and his mouth just moved wordlessly.

The woman pulled a phone from her pocket and tapped the screen a few times before holding it to her ear.

"This is Angelica, calling in. I've neutralized three Waifs here that will need to be bound and taken back to their Enclave." She paused for several moments and nodded.

"I don't believe there are any more here, the air only carries the scent of these three. Please direct a cleanup operation here. I have a minor injury so I won't be returning to the Hive tonight."

Liam realized that the woman's left arm was hanging limply at her side and blood had soaked through her coat and was dripping from her fingertips.

The woman's cheeks suddenly turned pink.

"Alaric, I'm fine. There is no need for you to be so worried. I just won't make the run back before the sun rises. I will find a place here to spend the day. One day of sleep will heal me up just fine and I will return in the evening."

Liam watched the woman pout and timidly raised his hand slightly.

"I, um, I mean, you could stay in my apartment, if you need somewhere to stay."

The woman immediately seized the opportunity.

"I've got a kid here, who was being chased by the Waifs, who says he has room for me at his place. It's right on my location and should be the perfect place to hide out for the day." After a few seconds of listening, she marched over to Liam and held her phone out to him.

"Speak up, kid."

Liam nervously took the phone and placed it to his ear.

"H-hello?".

A low, smooth voice answered him.

"Hello. I do hope Angelica is not causing you trouble. Are you certain it is alright for her to rest at your residence?"

Liam nodded.

"Y-yes. She saved me from the werewolves and got injured for it. I-it's the least I could do."

Angelica gave Liam a thumbs up.

"What is your name, young man?"

"Um. It's Liam. Liam Smith, sir."

"Liam, a good name. I am Alaric, Blood-bonded of Angelica. Is her injury very serious?"

Liam glanced at Angelica's shoulder again.

"I... um... don't think so. She fought two werewolves after she got hurt, so i-it doesn't seem too bad."

Liam heard a quiet sigh on the other side of the phone.

"Very Well. I will leave her in your care for now. Please ensure that she has what she needs. If she is overly difficult I promise we will compensate you for your troubles."

Liam quickly shook his head.

"N-no, there's no need for that. I'm happy to help."

Angelica took her phone back and put it to her ear.

"See? Everything will be fine here. Once the sun sets tonight I will return to the Hive."

She listened for a few more moments and sighed.

"I will." She spoke more softly now. "I promise I am okay."

She spared Liam a glance, pouting slightly.

"No, I am not bullying him. He is just a good kid."

Liam just stood silently, his back feeling cold against the apartment building door, not entirely sure what kind of conversation was happening between the two.

Angelica sighed one more time and turned away from Liam, lowering her voice.

"Please don't worry, My Love. It was just a single bite. It will heal quickly. Besides, there are still the Lords that will bc staying at the Enclave for the day. Even if something happened, they are very nearby."

Liam now felt like he was somehow intruding and tried his best to become part of the apartment building.

Angelica shook her head.

"Now you are just being silly. I am going to hang up now so we don't make the kid wait any longer. Goodbye, My Love."

Angelica groaned as she ended the call and slid her phone back into her pocket.

"My apologies." She said, turning back to Liam. "Alaric has a bad habit of worrying about everything, even when he doesn't need to. Sometimes especially when he doesn't need to"

Liam shook his head quickly.

"No, i-it's okay. I mean, I worry a lot too. I can understand."

Angelica glanced at her shoulder and then back at Liam with an almost embarrassed smile.

"Just do me a favor. If Alaric ever asks for specifics, don't tell him how bad it actually looks. It really will heal after a few hours of sleep, so he doesn't need to know. He will just worry needlessly."

Liam nervously nodded, not sure he could handle the stress of needing to lie.

Angelica smacked him on the shoulder with her good arm.

"Well, are we going in? Or are we staying outside for what little is left of the night?"

Liam jumped and fumbled around in his pockets, hurriedly looking for his keys.

* * *

Liam watched Angelica hold up the torn remains of her coat to inspect it, surprised that she was already able to lift her left arm again after only taking a short shower.

Angelica clicked her tongue and grumbled.

"Probably not worth trying to wash the blood out of." She said, tossing the coat on the floor next to a bloodstained towel. "Sorry for making a mess. I'll clean up before I leave tonight so it doesn't look like someone died in your shower."

Liam hurriedly shook his head.

"N-no, don't worry about it. It isn't a problem. I mean, no one else comes here. So no one would get the wrong idea or anything."

Angelica smirked, lowering herself down into an armchair in a dark corner. She adjusted her black vest and tugged at the left sleeve of her black dress shirt to ensure the holes in the shoulder wouldn't tear.

"You're just a whole bundle of nerves aren't you, kid? Are you sure you are alright having a strange woman sleeping in your apartment? There are many other places I could stay instead."

Liam tried not to make eye contact.

"I wouldn't say I'm particularly comfortable with it, but I don't think I have ever been comfortable with anything in my entire life. It doesn't really feel any different than a normal day and I would hate to put you through the trouble of finding somewhere else."

Angelica sighed.

"Well, I am Suite Lord Angelica. I suppose I should have properly introduced myself earlier. And, just in case you hadn't figured it out, I am a vampire. I hope that won't complicate matters."

Liam quickly shook his head.

"I-I thought you might be. I wouldn't think any normal person besides me would be dumb enough to be out during a full moon. And I'm not really worried about vampires more than anyone else. They don't usually attack people, I-I don't think. At least, that's what I was always told." Liam felt his heart rate increasing as he realized he was rambling again.

Angelica laughed.

"Relax and breathe kid, you're going to give yourself a heart attack. Biting people is a kind of personal thing for vampires. You can see other's memories when you bite them, so we don't do it unless we have permission or in self-defense. Plus, vampires are immune to most diseases but we don't have much of an immune system to fight them off. So if you ever do get bitten, you need to go straight to a hospital or it will be the infection that kills you, not the loss of blood."

Liam nodded nervously.

"G-good to know."

Angelica sighed and leaned her head back against the back of the chair.

"Ever try relaxation therapy? Breathing exercises? Heck, maybe calming incense?"

Liam nodded again.

"My mom sends me essential oils sometimes. They smell nice, but I've never really noticed much of a difference."

"Well, at least it sounds like your family is supportive. I suppose I should ask if you have any other questions. Anything that is going to bother you while I am here? I'll try to answer what I can. Hopefully, that will make you less likely to keel over while I am asleep."

Liam struggled to think of something, not wanting to be rude by not responding.

"Um, I guess I was wondering, or was just curious I guess, what it means to be Blood-bonded?"

Angelica chuckled, sounding a bit exasperated.

"Alaric is a royal pain in my nether regions. We have shared our blood with each other to form a bond between us."

Angelica pulled her shirt collar away from her neck, revealing two white scars on the left side of her neck.

"Among vampires, it essentially means we are married. Alaric doesn't spend a whole lot of time around Pure-Bloods and forgets they don't really know what it means."

"You called me that before. W-what is that?" Liam asked without thinking, his curiosity getting the best of him.

Angelica tilted her head forward to look at him for a moment.

"Oh, you mean Pure-Blood? Have you never heard the term before? It just means normal humans. Vampires and werewolves ended up the way they are because of a curse. Well, I guess that isn't exactly true. Vampires and werewolves share common ancestors. Those ancestors were cursed through means I am forbidden to speak of. The descendants of those ancestors inherited that curse, so we refer to ourselves as Curse-Bloods. Vampires and werewolves ended up as we are because of what we each did to mitigate the curse."

Liam nodded, finding this new information strangely fascinating.

"I see, that sounds kind of terrible."

Angelica laughed, shaking her head and waving her hand dismissively.

"Not really. I cannot speak for werewolves, but vampires suppressed our curse, to some extent, by making a deal with The Fey. Normally risky, even on a good day, but our elders happened to catch the King and Queen of The Fey in a good mood. So, aside from being unable to go out in sunlight and having an occasional sickness that causes a terrible thirst for blood, we can live relatively normal lives."

Liam nodded, his heart still pounding but he was, somehow, no longer feeling tense about having Angelica in the room.

"Is it normal for vampires to fight with werewolves?"

Angelica shook her head, leaning it back against the chair again.

"We are basically cousins, we work together all the time. What I was doing out there tonight wasn't fighting. I was protecting them from themselves. Though, I was a bit perturbed so I may have gone a bit overboard tonight."

Liam blinked in surprise.

"Protecting them from... themselves?"

Angelica nodded.

"When Waif and Alpha class werewolves transform they lose their sense of self and cannot control their desires or actions. Both vampires and werewolves have very strict laws to help protect Pure-Bloods and ourselves. Taking the life of a human, if not one hundred percent in self-defense, is an automatic death sentence. Most werewolves voluntarily isolate themselves, or lock themselves up, during a full moon. But there are a handful who don't, or who get out, or who are transforming for the first time and don't realize it.

As I am sure you already know, we usually mount a worldwide defense of major cities on full moon nights, to help keep those individuals from making a life-ending mistake. This year we even started getting help from The Academy, so there are a handful of sorcerers who have been lending us aid as well."

Liam nodded. He knew about The Academy of Sorcerers, and even knew a few sorcerers, but didn't really know enough about sorcery to know how helpful it would be against werewolves.

Angelica yawned and rubbed her left shoulder and Liam jumped.

"Oh, I'm sorry. I-I've kept you talking when I should be letting you rest."

Angelica waved him off.

"Don't worry about it, kid. I don't really like explaining stuff, but I enjoy talking to people. And I have twelve hours of daylight to sleep through, so it's not like I need to be in a hurry."

Liam shook his head.

"Still, I should let you rest. I-is there anything you need me to do for you? Should I cover my windows better?"

Angelica shook her head.

"No, your windows are pretty small and face another building. Just having the curtains drawn is enough. And I am perfectly comfortable in this chair. The best thing you can do is just to pretend I'm not even here and just go about your day normally. I'll get out of your hair as soon as the sun goes down."

Liam nodded and turned to go find his own bed, trying to decide whether or not he would be happier having a guest he didn't mind or having his apartment to himself again.

2

Chapter Two

Liam stood nervously, trying not to stare at the two slim men in black gothic tailcoats and black dress shirts standing by his front door.

"Alaric didn't need to have you guys stop here. I am perfectly capable of making it back to the Hive on my own." Angelica called from the bathroom where she was bundling up all the blood-stained towels in her long black coat. "Besides, I couldn't just leave such a large mess for the kid to clean up."

"I am sorry, Suite Lord, the Underlord asked us to check to make sure everything was alright. We didn't feel it right to return without you." The man who spoke stood quietly at attention, his hands clasped firmly behind his back.

Angelic wrapped her coat arms around the bundle and tied it shut.

"Don't be sorry, you're just trying to do what you think is expected of you. Just try and remember, Alaric isn't like Overlord Burchard. He will always tell you exactly what he wants you to do."

Angelica took her bundle and slung it over one shoulder.

"Though I am finished cleaning up here so, at this point, we might as well just head out together."

The two men bowed and one opened the front door.

Angelica patted Liam on the shoulder as she walked by, Liam doing his best not to jump.

"Thank you for the place to stay, kid. I will send you some new towels, so don't go wasting your money buying new ones just yet."

Liam quickly nodded.

"T-thanks. It was no problem."

Angelica waved behind her as she stepped out the front door.

"And try some meditation or something. I can hear your heart pounding from here. It is going to give out on you one of these days if you don't learn to relax."

Liam nodded again, unable to think of anything to say in return before the door was closed and they were gone.

After a few moments to try and get his heart rate to slow down, he carefully peeked into the bathroom.

For the most part, it seemed as if Angelica had done a good job cleaning up. Though, Liam could see there was a little bit of blood left in the sink that she had forgotten.

Liam opened the cupboard under the sink and pulled out a spray bottle and one of his last few wash rags. He sprayed the sink down and then went out to the kitchen to find a pair of rubber cleaning gloves.

As he passed by his front door, he felt a tingle run up his spine and into his neck. He paused for a moment and shuddered, not sure what had caused the feeling. After a few more moments, with no other similar feelings, he made his way into the kitchen and found his cleaning gloves.

Liam started back to the bathroom, pulling his gloves on, and was suddenly blown off his feet as his front door caved inward. He rolled a few times, grimacing as he accrued several bruises and felt a few splinters of wood digging into his arms where they were not covered by his gloves.

As he was trying to sit up to see what had happened, he heard a low growling sound. He froze, his eyes peering at the space where his door had been, and felt dread fill him as his brain slowly processed what he was seeing.

A large werewolf with thick black hair that was standing on end, and glowing blue eyes, filled the doorway. Its face was scrunched in an aggressive snarl, saliva dripping from its bared teeth.

The two sat quietly, staring at each other, for several moments. Liam watched the werewolf slowly start raking its claws along the floor, and he slowly bent one knee to get his leg underneath him.

After a few seconds, the werewolf leapt at Liam with a snarl and Liam pushed off the floor with his leg and rolled to the side, pulling himself into the bathroom.

The werewolf swiped, scrambling to claw at Liam, but slipped onto its side and slid past on the debris scattered along the hallway floor.

Liam rolled to his feet and slammed the bathroom door shut, forcing the bolt lock on the door into place and hoping it would hold up better than his front door had.

His hopes were quickly dashed as four long claws pierced the door, raking long gashes across the top of the door and ripping the top hinge from the frame. Another swipe broke off an entire corner of the door, and Liam could see the werewolf's jaws immediately trying to tear off more.

Liam looked around desperately, trying to find something to defend himself with, but there wasn't anything beyond the shower curtain and his cleaning supplies. He grabbed his cleaning spray from the sink, hoping that maybe he could get some in the werewolf's eyes and blind it long enough to let him make a run for the front door.

Another swipe ripped the bolt lock out of the wall and Liam quickly raised his spray bottle, but a searing blast of fire threw the werewolf away from the door with an inhuman shriek.

Liam thought he saw a black and red streak move past his vision and felt the whole apartment shudder with a heavy impact. There were several seconds of growling and snarling, along with crashing and sounds of glass breaking.

A few more seconds passed by, the walls shaking and a bright flash coming from somewhere in the apartment, then everything went still.

Liam stood frozen, not daring to move or get near the door. After a few moments, he heard someone speaking.

"Are you still here ki... um, Liam?"

Liam felt some amount of relief hearing Angelica's voice.

"I-I'm here." He stammered.

He heard footsteps kicking aside debris and then saw Angelica peer into the bathroom over what was left of the door.

"Oh, thank goodness you seem unharmed. Were you injured at all?"

Liam shook his head carefully.

"I-I don't think so. It happened so fast, I-I wasn't really thinking about what to do."

Angelica pushed what was left of the door open and motioned for Liam to come out.

"You did fine. You put something between you and him and that gave me enough time to get here. Come on, I can't let you stay here alone, it isn't safe."

Liam nodded, setting down his spray bottle and shakily stepping out into the hall. Angelica carefully turned him towards the front of the apartment and gently turned his head forward when he tried to look back over his shoulder.

"Best you don't look. I was... unkind."

Liam didn't argue, letting Angelica lead him outside the apartment building and under a street lamp where one of the men who had come for her was waiting.

"What of the other?" Angelica asked.

The man shook his head.

"Altus tried to contain him but, in the end, too much force was required."

Angelica nodded.

"I was worried that might be the case. Make sure both make it back to the Enclave. There are few werewolves who can change outside a full moon, and certainly not Waifs. Hopefully, Pack Leader Harklan can find out what happened. Then find any other Lord-class vampires still in the area and do a thorough search to see if there are any more. Also, ensure the apartment owner is notified and knows to appeal to the Enclave for compensation for the damages."

The man bowed.

"As you will, Suite Lord. What of the Pure-Blood?"

Angelica spared a glance at Liam.

"This is the fifth werewolf that has taken a specific interest in him in the last twenty-four hours. I don't like that and it doesn't feel like a coincidence. I am going to take him back to the Hive so that Alaric and Hivelord Andros can try and figure out what is happening."

The man bowed once more and then turned and disappeared into the shadows beyond the light cast by the street lamp.

Angelica watched him go, then put her arm gently around Liam's shoulders and pressed him forward.

"Come on. We have a long way to go tonight and part of the way you will have to be blindfolded. So we better get started."

Liam shuffled forward, trying to do as he was told while his brain struggled to fight through the shock of what had happened.

* * *

Liam stumbled along, trying to keep one hand on the cave wall to steady himself while Angelica led him carefully along holding the other.

"Did I tie your blindfold too tightly?" Angelica asked quietly, her voice echoing throughout the cave.

Liam tried to shake his head, promptly losing his bearings and bumping into the wall.

"No, it's fine. I'm just not very coordinated."

He heard Angelica scoff.

"I think you have plenty of coordination, I just don't think you realize it. You focus too much on other things and don't let your body act naturally."

Liam decided against shaking his head again.

"I've always been clumsy though, ever since I was a kid."

Liam felt the wall on his right disappear and he felt Angelica pull on his hand and lead him to the left. After a moment of fumbling, Liam found the wall again and they continued walking.

"And yet, when you were running from the werewolves last night, you sprinted halfway around a city block without a single stumble. And tonight you were light enough on your feet to avoid another and get to safety. That doesn't sound like someone who is naturally clumsy to me." Angelica spoke softly but with a hint of amusement in her voice.

Liam blinked a few times beneath his blindfold, unable to think of any argument to refute her claim.

After several more minutes of walking, they came to a stop and Angelica untied Liam's blindfold.

Liam blinked as a surprising amount of light filled his vision. After a few moments, his eyes adjusted and he found himself in a truly colossal open cavern.

Several rows of great stone columns, each column easily thirty feet across, reached up to support the cavern ceiling, and great arches spanned the space between them. Giant crystal chandeliers hung from each arch, scattering a gentle white light across everything below. The ground was lined with strips of dim lights that indicated the paths that lead throughout the cavern.

Numerous buildings of many descriptions were scattered among the columns and the lit paths wound between them, occasionally branching off and disappearing into various tunnels.

Angelica motioned for Liam to follow her, and she led him towards a large building set on a section of stone that was elevated above the rest of the main cavern.

She opened a door and ushered Liam inside, taking him through to a second door and leading him into a large conference room.

Angelica pulled a chair out at the end of the large glass table that dominated the room and waved Liam over to sit.

"Take a seat, I'm going to go let them know we are here. Just try to relax. I promise that neither of the individuals who are coming to meet you are intimidating in the slightest."

After Liam sat down, Angelica nodded once and then rushed back out through the door. He sat quietly in the silence of the conference room, trying to breathe slowly and consciously relax his muscles.

A few minutes later Liam heard the door open and Angelica entered the room again, followed by a young-looking man, with silver hair that reached the back of his neck, who was wearing a red suit and tailcoat with black trim. He stood a few inches taller than Angelica and suddenly Liam felt like the air in the room had grown much heavier.

"This is Underlord Alaric, my Blood-bonded." Angelica stated, motioning to the man.

Liam stood quickly and bowed slightly, feeling like the weight of the air around him would squeeze all the air out of his lungs.

"I-it's a pleasure to meet you, sir." He stuttered.

Alaric chuckled, returning the bow and then holding out his hand.

"And a pleasure to meet you, young Liam. Despite the circumstances, I am glad I get to thank you in person for taking care of Angelica."

Liam nervously accepted the handshake with a nod, feeling like a heavy pack had been placed on his shoulders to weigh him down.

"I-I didn't really do much, but I was happy to help."

Alaric smiled and walked around to a seat nearby.

"Hopefully we will be able to return the favor, and offer you our help in turn."

Angelica walked around to the other side and pulled out a chair for herself, leaning over to Liam.

"You can sit down again."

Liam twitched and hurriedly sat back down in his chair and turned to face the table.

"Now, I cannot make any promises until Hivelord Andros arrives and we receive permission to act, but I have a few suspicions as to what could be happening." Alaric said, pressing a button on the side of the table and causing the glass surface to light up.

"Firstly, I would like to perform a quick test. Have you ever had your blood drawn before?"

Liam nodded slowly.

Alaric nodded back and pulled a small box out of his pocket and placed it on the table.

"We won't need to draw any venous blood, just a drop from a prick in the finger. A bit like testing your blood sugar. Would you be comfortable with allowing me to do that?"

Liam could feel himself wringing his hands together and tried to force himself to relax.

"T-that's okay with me. If it will help you."

Alaric smiled, opening the small box and putting on a pair of latex gloves.

"I am hoping that we will be helping you. Are you right-handed or left-handed?"

"Um, right-handed."

Alaric nodded, pulling out a single use packet containing an alcohol wipe.

"Then let's use your left hand if you will."

Liam nodded and nervously held out his left hand. Alaric opened the wipe and then used it to carefully wipe down the fingers on Liam's left hand. Then he pulled out a glass slide and a small, capped needle.

"I know most people don't care for needles, so if you need to look away you may do so. Just try to relax and I'll make this as painless as I can."

Liam nodded, opting to squeeze his eyes shut. He felt Alaric grasp the two middle fingers on his left hand and turn them palm up. After a moment, he felt a slight prick on his ring finger, somewhere between the side of his finger and the pad on the front. The pain disappeared almost instantly, and Liam slowly opened his eyes.

Alaric was now holding the glass slide beside Liam's pricked finger. With a gentle squeeze, a single small drop of blood was pushed out of the small hole made by the needle and onto the slide.

Alaric gently sat the slide on the table and then wiped Liam's finger off with a cotton ball before spraying it with a small spray bottle.

"There, all done. The spray should heal the wound so you won't bleed anymore. It may be slightly sore for a day or two but, hopefully, the pain was tolerable."

Liam nodded, inspecting his fingers.

"I-it wasn't as bad as I expected. It's like the pain was gone before I realized it hurt."

Alaric chuckled.

"I am glad to hear it. I strive to ensure that our guests do not have to go through more pain than is necessary."

Liam nodded slowly, not sure what that meant.

"Alaric, really, you need to give context if you are going to say things like that." Angelica stated.

Alaric frowned.

"I am sorry Angie, please explain for me."

Angelica sighed.

"We generally don't have guests here very often. This Hive has to remain secret for reasons I can't explain. When we do have guests, we have to lead them here blindfolded like I did you. Now, the only reason we would bring guests here is if someone in the Hive needs blood. Again, that doesn't really happen often, since the only time we really need blood is if we get very sick or are severely injured. Most things we can just recover from, like I did at your apartment. But to recover from severe injuries we require blood. We ask people to donate blood willingly, and we bring them here and they donate it the same way you would to a hospital or blood bank. When Alaric says he wants to avoid causing the guests pain, he means when we are drawing blood. We don't beat up our guests."

Liam nodded, feeling like some of the weight that had been piling up on him was starting to lessen.

"I-I understand. That makes sense."

Angelica grumbled, leaning back in her chair and crossing her arms over her chest.

"This is why I don't like explaining things, My Love. I feel like I just talked the kid's ear off and only explained very little."

Alaric lifted the glass slide carefully and held the drop of blood at eye level, his eyes seeming to peer through it.

"I apologize if I caused any confusion. My responsibilities to the Hive often prevent me from leaving. I rarely get to interact with other people outside."

"You could get out more if you wished, Alaric." A voice interjected from the doorway. "We are never so busy we could not spare you for a few days."

Everyone turned to see an older, clean-shaven man with medium-length silver hair to match Alaric's. He wore a long black coat with red sleeves, buttons, and trim.

Angelica stood and bowed, Liam quickly following suit.

"Good evening, Hivelord." Angelica stated simply.

The older man nodded and made his way around to the head of the table.

"Good evening, Angelica. I am glad to see you have returned to us healthy and whole. And you must be the young man who helped our dear Angelica."

Liam nodded carefully and sat down when Angelica did.

"I-I am Liam, sir. A pleasure to meet you."

The Hivelord lowered himself into his seat.

"Likewise. I am sure Alaric has already expressed our appreciation for your cooperation, but please allow me to repeat it. We are grateful for your willingness to harbor one of our own when she was injured. As such, we hope that we will be able to repay your kindness."

Liam hurriedly shook his head.

"I-I was happy to help. She saved me. It was the least I could do."

Liam heard Angelica sigh heavily.

"Just let them do what they want. Neither one of us will ever convince them not to. Trust me. I have tried."

Liam frowned, not sure how to respond.

The Hivelord chuckled.

"Neither Alaric, nor myself, like to leave people unrewarded for their efforts. Consider it the longstanding habit of two old men."

The Hivelord turned to Alaric.

"Well, do you believe your suspicion was correct?"

Alaric nodded once, inspecting the drop of blood for a few more moments before lowering it slightly and taking a deep breath through his nose. A wave of gold played across his bright blue eyes.

"I think it is very likely, though we should consult with Master Shepherd just the same."

The Hivelord nodded and turned back to Angelica.

"Were the Waifs you encountered this evening the same as the ones you met during the full moon?"

Angelica shook her head, frowning.

"No, the three we encountered last night were returned to the enclave. Last night was just like any other normal full moon. The two we encountered tonight were far more aggressive and more resilient. We were not able to subdue them like normal and, unfortunately, both lost their lives."

The Hivelord nodded sadly.

"I see. Was there anything else you noticed about them? Anything different at all?"

Angelica shook her head again.

"I'm sorry Hivelord. I didn't notice anything. They smelled the same as normal Waifs. Their transformations were normal, outside of not being during a full moon or Hunt."

Liam thought about it for a moment while Angelica spoke and then timidly raised his hand.

"Um…" He paused, not certain if he should speak.

"Did you notice something, young man?" The Hivelord asked politely.

Liam carefully nodded.

"Um, the two I encountered face to face had different colored eyes. I don't know if that is significant or not."

Alaric sat up straighter and carefully set the glass slide back down on the table.

"How were they different?"

Liam carefully wrung his hands together, squeezing them between his knees.

"Um, the one I met in the alley last night had these really sharp yellow eyes. The one that broke into my apartment today had really intense blue eyes that almost seemed like they might have been… glowing?"

Alaric and the Hivelord shared a concerned look.

"And you are sure of this?"

Liam nodded silently.

Alaric leaned forward and tapped on the glass table, waking up the screen and opening a menu.

"I will contact Master Shepherd, and then I think I will take you up on your previous offer, Hivelord. I may need to leave the Hive for a day to investigate the Enclave."

The Hivelord nodded and waved one hand.

"Your leave is granted."

* * *

Angelica sat quietly, watching Alaric's back as he carefully wrote a letter on simple letter paper.

"You have been quiet." Alaric stated quietly, his pen never pausing. "Do you regret what happened?"

Angelica frowned, an unhappy sigh escaping her as lips quivered.

"It has been so long since my hand was forced. I can't help but feel like I could have done something more to save him."

"Indeed?" Alaric asked, setting down his pen and opening a drawer in his desk. "Do you think you could have controlled the Waif with lesser force?"

Angelica looked down at her hands, hearing Alaric moving paper around from the desk.

"I don't know. I tried to hold back."

"I believe you did, Angie."

Angelica watched Alaric's hand grasp hers and he carefully pulled her until she stood.

"You have always had a careful hand." Alaric lifted Angelica's hand to his lips and kissed it. "Altus was also unable to subdue the Waif he encountered. I am certain that you did all in your power to protect him. Young Liam survived because of your quick action."

Angelica frowned, and then Alaric gently lifted her chin so she would look him in the eye.

"Do not let the life that was lost make you forget the lives that were saved." Alaric smiled gently. "In the end, all our effort is to protect those who need our strength."

Angelica did her best to smile back.

"I only wish I could do more. Perhaps I could escort young Liam to Koyane Manor. I would like to make sure he is able to arrive safely."

Alaric's smile turned into a grin, exposing his clean white teeth and fangs.

"I thought you might feel that way." He held up a freshly sealed envelope. "I would like you to deliver this to the Master of the Manor. Master Shepherd has already agreed to let them know you are coming."

Angelica took the envelope and carefully hugged Alaric.

"You do too much." She sighed. "Thank you."

She felt Alaric's arms reach around her and hold her tight.

"Anything for you is never too much." He told her. "But when you go, there are some things I want you to ask them."

3

Chapter Three

Liam watched Angelica pull a small case from her pocket as they sat in the back of a car with blacked-out windows. She opened it and pulled a small vial and a short triangular-shaped object.

"What is that?" Liam asked, uncomfortable from the long and silent drive

Angelica took the vial and clamped the triangular object to the top, twisting it to screw it down tight.

"It's a special medication. It will let me walk out in the daylight for a while. We can't expect everyone else to cater to our shortcomings."

Angelica tightened the top on the vial and then twisted it in the opposite direction. The triangular section detached and revealed it had been covering a small needle.

"So, could you have used it before? Instead of staying at my apartment, I mean."

Angelica lifted the vial and pressed the needle into the side of her neck. The vial hissed as pressure was released, and her eyes flashed with a dim blue light for a few moments before returning to their usual green.

"It was an option." She said, putting a plastic cap over the needle and returning it to the small case. "But it was better to rest and heal from my injury instead. Besides, the medicine is rare and difficult to make. It's also hard on the body. More than two injections in a given twenty-four hour period will kill most vampires, so we try to avoid using it when possible."

Liam frowned.

"That sounds dangerous. How long does it last? Are you going to be okay?"

Angelica laughed.

"Relax kid, I've used this many times before. It's not exactly pleasant, but it isn't any cause for concern. It has an effective use time of about six to eight hours. More than enough to take you to visit Koyane Manor and get back to the Hive. And any minor effects it might have I can just sleep off when I get back."

Liam looked down at his feet, wringing his hands together.

"W-what kind of place is Koyane Manor?"

Angelica slipped the small case into her new, red-trimmed, black coat and leaned back in her seat.

"You know what an Aspect is, don't you?" She asked.

Liam thought for a moment and then nodded slowly.

"I think so. Isn't it someone who has some kind of connection to an animal?"

Angelica glanced over at Liam.

"How can you be wrong but right at the same time?"

Liam just continued to stare at his feet, not sure how to answer.

Angelica sighed, crossing her arms over her chest.

"Aspects are humans who have inherited blood from an animal somewhere in their family line. Either through a blessing from an animal spirit, or from a powerful or magical creature who was capable of taking human form. An Aspect can come from pretty much any animal you can think of, though some are more powerful than others. It just depends on how much blood was inherited and how well it mixes with the blood of the person who carries it."

Liam nodded slowly, thinking back to what had happened the night before at the hive with Alaric.

"Do... Does Alaric think I might be an Aspect?"

Angelica glanced at Liam from the corner of her eye, a slight smile twisting her expression into a smirk.

"You're a lot more observant than you look, kid. I didn't even figure out what he wanted to check you for until he mentioned speaking to Master Shepherd. Koyane Manor is the name of a large number of mansions and estates all over the world belonging to a powerful diplomat and businessman of the same name. He mostly employs individuals with blood Aspects. Master Shepherd runs the day-to-day business of the estates and watches over the people in Master Koyane's employ. Though, you won't be meeting directly with Master Shepherd today. He usually operates out of the main manor house in Utah."

Liam blinked a few times.

"The main manor is in Utah?"

Angelica laughed.

"Seems strange, doesn't it, for a man born in Japan. Utah seems like a pretty empty and unassuming desert, but there is a great deal of power concentrated there. Along with Koyane Manor's main house, there is also one of the largest branches of The Academy of Sorcerers. Many of the most skilled sorcerers in the world have trained there. People there are just quiet and peaceful, so nobody ever even thinks of what they could actually be capable of if they were forced to act. Actually, perhaps it is for the best if people don't think about it."

Liam felt the car turn onto an unpaved surface and Angelica shifted in her seat.

"We have arrived. Don't worry about anything. They go out of their way to be extremely polite here." Angelica said, pulling a pair of dark sunglasses out of her coat and putting them on.

After a few moments, the car slowed and came to a stop. Angelica put her hand on the door handle and paused for a moment. She grumbled for a few seconds and then opened the door, bright sunlight flooding into the car.

Liam quickly opened his own door and followed her out.

"Ugh, I always forget how bright the sun is." Angelica complained, shading her eyes with one hand.

Liam quickly walked around the car, looking up at the sky.

"It is a very clear morning too."

"It's gross." Angelica whined, then turned and started walking away.

Liam followed for a few steps before looking up and seeing the mansion for the first time and freezing.

The mansion was easily two or three times the size of the apartment building he lived in, and could easily have filled the giant main cavern of the Hive they had just left.

Liam felt a hand on his shoulder and shook himself.

"Let's keep moving." Angelica said, gently pulling him forward. "I can stand in the sun for now, but I would still rather not."

Liam hurriedly nodded and followed, doing his best to look at Angelica's back instead of the mansion.

As they neared the front door they were met by a butler, an older gentleman with graying hair and dressed in a clean suit and tailcoat. He bowed deeply at the waist.

"Welcome. What brings you to Koyane Manor on this fine day?"

Angelica nodded politely and then pulled an envelope from one of her pockets.

"We are visiting from The Great Plains Hive. I have a letter of introduction from Underlord Alaric asking us to visit at the instruction of Master Shepherd."

The butler accepted the envelope with another bow.

"I see. Master Shepherd did tell us to expect guests. I didn't realize we would be graced by the presence of a Vampire Lord. Please, come inside. I am sure the sunlight is not comfortable for you."

The butler stepped aside and waved them in.

Angelica nodded and walked through the doors into a large foyer, Liam close behind.

"Please wait here a moment and I will announce your arrival."

The butler bowed once more and walked away, disappearing through a nearby door.

They stood quietly, Liam nervously shifting his weight from one foot to another. After a few moments, they were approached by a young girl, who was no more than ten, with curly blonde hair wearing a maid outfit and carrying a tray.

"Would you like something to drink?" She asked timidly, holding up the tray which had two glasses of iced tea balanced on it.

Angelica smiled, though she never let her teeth show.

"Why thank you. I was just thinking I was feeling a bit thirsty."

Angelica took one of the glasses and took a sip, sighing as if she hadn't had anything to drink in days.

"This is just what I needed. Thank you, little one."

The young girl blushed and turned to Liam with the tray.

Liam nervously took the other glass, not wanting to be rude.

"T-thank you." He said with a slight bow, making sure to take a sip from the glass.

The young girl turned the tray and held it against her chest, bowing as best as she could.

"Please let me know if you need anything else."

The little girl stumbled through the words, suggesting she had been told what to say and was still trying to learn how to say it. Then she turned and rushed out of the room.

Angelica half smiled.

"Cute maid."

Liam just nodded in agreement and absently took another sip from his glass.

After several minutes of waiting, which felt like an eternity to Liam, the butler returned.

"Please follow me, Lady Angelica. Master Liam."

Angelica placed her half-finished iced tea on a small table and Liam did the same, quickly following behind.

They made their way down a long hall and up a flight of stairs, which led to another long hall. At the end of the hall, they were ushered through a heavy oak door and into a large office.

The office was lined with shelves of books on all sides. The rest of the room was fairly bare, containing only a large desk and two armchairs placed in front of it for guests. Behind the desk sat a slim woman with chestnut brown hair and brown eyes that looked like the rings of a tree.

The woman was reading a letter in one hand and motioned with the other.

"Please, have a seat."

Angelica gracefully slipped across the room and smoothly lowered herself into one of the chairs. Liam followed suit, though much more stiffly.

After a few moments of reading, the woman placed the letter on her desk and folded her hands together.

"Allow me to introduce myself. I am Olivia Tenison, and I am the Master of this branch house of Koyane Manor. A pleasure to meet both of you. To move directly onto business, Master Shepherd informed me that there was someone who needed our aid who would be visiting us today."

Olivia motioned to the letter on the desk.

"This letter from Underlord Alaric expands on that. He states, among other things, that young Master Liam here may have an Aspect of Blood. He wishes us to look into it and take him under our wings if that is the case."

Olivia turned to Liam.

"This, of course, is up to you. You must decide if you wish us to discover your Aspect if, indeed, you have one. And you must also decide whether you wish to stay with us here and learn to live with your Aspect, or return to your home and live your life normally. We will not ask you to give up your free will here, so the decision is yours alone."

Liam frowned, feeling like a heavy weight was suddenly placed on his shoulders. After a moment he glanced at Angelica.

Angelica shook her head at him.

"I can't tell you what to do, kid. You have to make your own choice. Maybe start by asking yourself, 'Do I want to continue living like I am? Or do I want to make a change?'."

Liam stared down at his hands, wringing them together nervously. After a few minutes of thought, he slowly nodded.

"I... I want to know if I have an Aspect. And I would like to stay here. I-if you will have me."

Olivia smiled, reaching out and picking up an old corded phone from its receiver. She placed it to her ear and pressed a button.

"Please send Oliver to me."

Olivia hung up the phone.

"If you do have an Aspect, we will help you learn what it means. And you will always be welcome here."

Olivia picked up the letter again and sighed.

"I am not sure how much help we will be in regards to your other query, however."

Angelica nodded.

"That is quite all right, Mistress Olivia. Alaric already understands that your knowledge may not be much greater than our own. He hopes, however, that hearing what you know from your perspective will shed more light on the subject. Anything you can tell us will be helpful."

Olivia nodded and set the letter aside once more.

"It is entirely possible for an Aspect to take on the form of an animal. This, I am sure, you know well since werewolves are, by all definitions, Aspects. However, the Resonance of Blood must be exceptionally pure to be able to achieve such a thing."

Liam felt his curiosity rising and spoke without thinking.

"Does that mean werewolves have that kind of resonance?"

Olivia shook her head.

"No, werewolves do not have a strong resonance with their Aspect. If we were to put a number to it, most fall somewhere between eighteen and twenty-six percent. An Aspect must have a Blood Resonance of between sixty and seventy percent to achieve a partial transformation, and over ninety percent for a full transformation. It has been a very long time since any Aspect has had that level of Resonance." Olivia unconsciously glanced over at her phone as she finished speaking.

Angelica nodded, half a smile tugging at her lips as she noticed Olivia's glance.

"Okay, so then is it their Cursed Blood that changes things?"

Olivia nodded in return.

"Yes. At least as far as we understand. Specifically during a full moon, or a Wild Hunt, the Cursed Blood corrupts both the human blood and the Aspect. This forces both to mix together, making their resonance effectively one hundred percent for a short time. The exception to this rule, of course, are the Archon Class werewolves who can transform at will. However, they do so by manipulating their own Cursed Blood, not by a natural resonance with their Aspect."

Angelica shifted her position and crossed her legs.

"That makes a good deal of sense. Then, them being Aspects, would having your own Aspect change how they react to you?"

Olivia folded her hands together again.

"There have been instances where certain predatory Aspects feel aggression towards Aspects that would naturally be considered prey to that Aspect. Though that has rarely ever amounted to more than moderate bullying."

Angelica looked back and forth between Olivia and Liam a few times, the wheels in her brain turning.

"What if the predatory Aspect had lost themselves to bloodlust and was unable to make rational decisions? Do you think they may prefer a prey Aspect over a regular person?"

Olivia tilted her head to one side in thought. After a few moments, as understanding began to dawn on her, she looked over at Liam.

"It is not something I think we could verify, or would ever wish to, but... I do not think it is outside the realm of possibility."

Angelica smirked, clearly seeing Alaric's grin in her mind, and shaking her head.

"That man will be the end of me, I swear. He could just tell us what he is thinking."

Olivia slowly nodded, realizing the purpose of the questions.

"Master Shepherd and Master Orpheus both hold Lord Alaric in high regard. At times like this, it is easy to see why."

Angelica scoffed.

"I think he is too smart for his own good." Angelica's expression softened and seemed almost sad. "Makes me feel a bit..."

She paused for a moment, then shook herself.

"No, not letting myself go there."

Olivia smiled at Angelica knowingly, but a knock at the door interrupted any further discussion.

"Come in."

The door opened and a thin young man with sandy-colored hair stepped inside.

"You called for me, Mistress Olivia?"

Olivia nodded and motioned for the young man to come forward.

"I would like you to look into this young man's heart and see what, if any, Aspect lies within him."

The young man made his way over to stand in front of Liam and held out one hand.

"Hello. My name is Oliver, I would be honored if you would allow me to see your Aspect."

Liam nervously accepted the handshake.

"I'm Liam. N-nice to meet you. I would be grateful if you could tell me... what I am, I guess."

Oliver shook Liam's hand and nodded.

"That's my job. Please relax and allow me to look into your heart. Now, please forgive me."

Oliver placed his hands on either side of Liam's head and tilted his face upward, leaning in close and staring directly into his eyes.

Liam tensed up as Oliver's eyes slowly turned a bright yellow, and his pupils stretched into long slits.

"Relaxsss." Oliver spoke quietly, drawing out the word in a long hiss.

Liam felt his vision blur and his body felt like gelatin. Everything around him appeared like he was looking through oily water. Everything except for Oliver's sharp yellow eyes, which filled the center of his vision and demanded to have all attention.

What felt like hours passed by and then, in a moment of clarity, Liam saw a flash of black and brown scales and he jerked upright, pulling away from Oliver.

Oliver stood upright slowly, looking down at his empty hands.

"I've never had anyone break away from me that quickly before."

"Were you not able to see clearly?" Olivia asked, clearly concerned with what had happened.

Oliver turned and faced the desk.

"No, I saw him very clearly, Mistress Olivia. He is a powerful Zodiac. Specifically, he is a Rabbit Aspect."

Angelica laughed out loud, quickly covering her mouth to try and hide her grin.

"A rabbit? I've never heard a more perfect thing in my entire life. I knew you seemed quick on your feet and that twitchy disposition of yours makes sense now too."

Liam looked down at his hands sheepishly.

Olivia sat back in her chair, relieved.

"Well, I wouldn't have thought a Zodiac Aspect would walk into my office today. You have a very special bloodline, Master Liam."

Liam looked up at Olivia, unable to think of anything to say.

"Oliver, please take Master Liam and have Master Tanaka prepare a room for him. Then I would like you to show him around the manor and help him learn where everything is. I will contact Master Shepherd and ask how he would like to proceed."

Olivia turned to Liam.

"Please feel free to ask Oliver any questions you have. For the time being, just try to relax and become accustomed to the manor. I am sure Master Shepherd will be excited to hear about you and will do his best to ensure you will receive the training and education befitting your Aspect. If you need anything, or wish to contact anyone, please let us know and we will ensure you are accommodated. And allow me to be the first to say, Welcome to Koyane Manor."

Liam shook himself and carefully stood, his head swimming in a sea of thoughts. As he followed Oliver, he felt a hand grab his arm. He looked back to see Angelica smiling up at him from her chair.

"I'm glad you found yourself. Don't think about it too much. Try to let yourself act naturally and you will be fine. And don't forget to try and relax." Angelica let go of Liam's arm and waved. "Feel free to send us a Christmas card or something. Alaric would be glad to hear from you."

Liam nodded, feeling a very slight amount of his tension lifting.

"Thank you, for watching out for me. I'm glad I got to meet you, Angelica."

Liam bowed slightly and then turned and followed Oliver out of the room.

Once the door had closed behind them, Angelica rubbed one eye under her dark glasses.

"Stupid kid, making me want to feel all weepy. I bet Alaric knew this would happen. He is probably laughing to himself about it right now. I won't let him hear the end of it."

Olivia smiled.

"We will take care of Liam here. Of that, I can assure you. Was there anything else you would need of us today? Aside from the questions you had asked?"

Angelica shook her head and stood.

"No, I really only just came to escort the kid and make sure he was alright. Though your insight was useful, so thank you. I will relay what you said back to Alaric."

Olivia nodded.

"Very well. Please, do call on us again if you have any need. It was a pleasure to meet you."

Angelica waved, walking towards the door.

"Likewise. Hopefully I can convince Alaric to come and visit in person next time."

Angelica placed her hand on the door handle and paused for a moment.

"Actually, might I ask one more question before I go? Perhaps it is a bit of a selfish question, but something came to mind while we spoke and I am curious."

Olivia nodded again.

"Of course."

Angelica glanced back over her shoulder.

"When you said that it had been a long time since any Aspect had had a strong enough Resonance of Blood to change, that wasn't entirely true, was it?"

Olivia blinked in surprise and Angelica smirked.

"Alaric and the kid aren't the only ones who can observe and make connections."

Olivia nodded slowly.

"I cannot say for certain. In all honesty, Lord Alaric may be more qualified to answer than I. What I can say is that, in living memory, there has not been a more powerful Aspect than Master Shepherd. And as a sorcerer, only Master Orpheus and Lord Alaric could rival him."

Angelica nodded, her smirk softening into a smile.

"Alaric views them both almost like younger brothers. Well, much much younger brothers. I always feel a bit like I am prying if I ask him about them, so I just wanted to verify my suspicions with you."

Angelica turned the door handle and opened the door a crack.

"That said, you should also not hesitate to ask if you ever need anything too. Alaric and I will happily help you if you ever have the need. And since I know Master Shepherd at least well enough to know he likely won't ask himself, I will leave it to you to call on us if the need arises."

Olivia smiled pleasantly.

"I will bear that in mind. Your kindness is appreciated."

Angelica waved once more and then disappeared through the door, leaving Olivia to lift the phone at her desk once again. She dialed a few numbers and sat back in her chair.

"Good morning, Lady Tanya. I have news for Master Shepherd. Koyane Manor has gained a new Zodiac Aspect."

4

Chapter Four

Alaric crouched next to the body of a young man with blonde hair. He carefully lifted one of the deceased man's eyelids and frowned at what he saw.

"Is something wrong, Underlord?" A large man with gray hair leaned against a desk nearby, watching Alaric go about his inspection.

"It may well be, but I will need more information to be sure." Alaric responded, carefully brushing the man's eyes closed again. "I am sorry that we were unable to bring your charges back to you alive, Harklan. My sincere condolences."

The large man waved him off.

"Don't concern yourself with that, Underlord. As they were, they would have taken the lives of others and their fate would have been the same. The actions of your people saved lives, that is what is important. Every Curse-Blood here understands that, and they would rather be killed than be allowed to take another's life."

Alaric carefully turned over the man's hand, noting a lack of rigor mortis.

"All the same, Angelica returned to the Hive with unshed tears in her eyes. It breaks her heart that this was necessary, though she is too proud to show it."

Harklan sighed, folding his large arms over his thick chest.

"You and your Wife feel too much empathy for us. Far too much for individuals of your power and influence."

Alaric held one hand over the young man's chest and a subtle golden glow surrounded him as he allowed a small amount of power to flow through him.

"Who we are is of no consequence. My responsibility is to ensure that everyone can live peacefully. Be they Curse-Blood or Pure-Blood. From the greatest of us to the very least. You, and the members of your Enclave, are no exception."

Alaric looked up at Harklan with a polite smile.

"Besides, it is Angie's empathy and heart that drew me to her. Even after so many decades, she still surpasses my every expectation. If we can continue to serve in such a capacity, we shall both be happy."

Harklan harrumphed.

"You are one of the least unpleasant Vampires I have ever met. I don't think I care for it much."

Alaric laughed, standing upright.

"I will take that as a compliment." He looked down at the body as he spoke. "You said the other was worse off?"

Harklan nodded.

"My doctor did an autopsy on both, but he said the second man was badly burned and there was much less information to be gleaned."

Alaric smiled sadly.

"That does sound like Angie's work. Were the other three who were returned to you badly injured?"

Harklan shook his head.

"No. Pretty beat up, a bit of singed hair, but nothing they won't recover from in a couple of days. At least physically. I hear Suite Lord Angelica is a force of nature in a fight. I would be willing to bet those three lock themselves up extra tight for the next full moon."

Alaric chuckled.

"She carries her element well. I imagine most would find her intense, to say the least."

This managed to entice a grin out of Harklan.

"I respect that. Most of you vampires are stuffy at best. Having one of you who can speak their mind and get their hands dirty is refreshing. Though, as far as vampires go, you also seem to speak plainly. Makes things simple."

Alaric smiled.

"I've lived long enough to know that simple is best. I try to avoid the political climate that surrounds the Elders and Hivelords. I am sure you have to play your fair share of games among the other Enclaves."

Harklan growled.

"Got a lot of young pups running around these days. Some of them have a hard time understanding why we do things the way we do. Guess that is one of the benefits to your long life, not having to relearn everything every new generation."

Alaric nodded.

"Perhaps. Though we still have young ones, and some not so young ones, who occasionally want to change things."

"And how do you handle the stubborn ones?" Harklan asked, pushing himself away from the desk as a knock sounded at the door.

Alaric turned to watch the large man walk across the room, making a fist.

"I suspect in much the same way you do."

Harklan laughed loudly, opening the door to reveal a surprised-looking man in a white coat, carrying a file folder.

"Hey Doc, what's up?"

The man cleared his throat.

"I brought the results from the tests we ran from the autopsies. There were several drugs and a few other chemicals I didn't recognize in both their systems."

"Might I take a look?" Alaric asked.

Harklan stepped aside and waved the doctor in.

"Doc, meet Underlord Alaric of the Great Plains Hive. Underlord, this is our resident doctor, Dorian Alstead."

The doctor entered the room and bowed.

"It is an honor to meet you, Underlord."

Alaric bowed in return.

"Likewise. What specifically did you find in your autopsy, Doctor?"

The doctor opened his folder and pulled out a handful of printed pages, holding them out to Alaric. Alaric accepted the pages and began reading.

The doctor turned slightly so he could see both Alaric and Harklan.

"Aside from the expected injuries and cause of death, we found several drugs, including amphetamines and opioids, in the system of both men. Looking at the doses found, most likely they had been using them recreationally. However, there was also an exceptionally high dose of Prednisone and lesser doses of Tacrolimus and Cyclosporine."

Alaric glanced up from the papers.

"Anti-rejection drugs?"

The doctor nodded.

"Yes, though I can only guess at why they were there. Aside from that, there were several other things I believe were likely fillers in whatever they were taking, though I should note there were also trace amounts of silver found in their blood that I cannot reasonably explain."

"Silver?" Harklan grumbled, clearly unhappy.

The doctor nodded again.

"It was not much, certainly not enough to kill them, but it was enough that they would have definitely been aware of it being there. I don't know why they would have taken it, though there were a handful of chemicals in their blood that I am not familiar with. It is possible that they took something else, and the silver came from that.

Unfortunately, I also don't think that we can ignore the possibility of their drugs being laced with silver if their identity as werewolves was known. Fear of werewolves is at an all-time low, but that is no guarantee that someone wouldn't attack them anyway."

Harklan frowned but, out of the corner of his eyes, he saw an expression on Alaric's face that caused even the large werewolf to feel the hair on the back of his neck stand up.

Alaric pulled out the second page of the stack and handed the rest back to the doctor.

"Forget you ever saw this report, doctor. However, if you do ever run into something like this again, report it directly to Harklan and then to me. You are dismissed." Alaric's tone left no room for disagreement.

The doctor stuffed the papers into his folder and bowed, quickly turning and leaving the room without another word.

Alaric waved one hand towards the door, and the bolt lock slid shut. He held out the page he had taken to Harklan.

"What have you been told about The Great Plains Hive?"

Harklan took the page and looked down at it, seeing a graph of some sort, and labels explaining each spike on the graph. A small number of those spikes were labeled with question marks.

"I know it is the second largest Hive in the world, with well over a thousand active vampires. The Great Plains Hive also coordinates all business of all continental American hives, and is in charge of all imports and exports for those vampires."

Alaric nodded slowly.

"That is correct, but there is something else. Something far more important. Something I am certain you will keep secret if I share it with you."

Harklan slowly lowered the page, recognizing the sound of a threat in Alaric's voice.

"I am certain I have no choice in the matter, but you have my silence. Does it have to do with what was in my charges' blood?"

Alaric nodded again.

"Deep underground, below the Great Plains Hive, is a crystal formation. It was formed by an ancient wellspring of raw energy that used to flow up from the earth there. The power that was there is gone, drawn away by leylines that have long since also run dry. But what remains is a solid formation of what amounts to this world's life-blood. We call it, Quintessence."

Harklan knew enough about sorcery to know that what Alaric was talking about was exceptional, but he also knew he likely didn't appreciate the full scope of this revelation.

Alaric continued.

"Quintessence, in its raw form, is incredibly potent. So much so that it is virtually unusable for anything other than sorcery. However if diluted, and mixed with other minerals, it becomes a powerful medication that allows vampire kind to walk under the sun."

Harklan felt his eyebrows raise.

"Something that can combat your Curse and your Fey Contract? So that's how you vampires have been able to visit the Enclave during daylight hours."

Alaric nodded his head.

"It is only a temporary solution. It lasts a mere few hours, and injecting repeated doses quickly becomes fatal to even the most powerful vampires."

Harklan looked back down at the paper in his hand.

"Is one of these chemicals the doctor couldn't identify Quintessence?"

Alaric stared at the page for a few moments.

"I cannot say for certain, but it looks remarkably similar. And an eyewitness account claimed noticing side effects of using the drug. There are a few problems if that is the case though. Firstly, the drug we vampires use is useless to werewolves. When we first discovered the Quintessence we attempted to create a version that could help keep werewolves from transforming on full moons, or at least allow them to maintain their faculties. Those attempts, however, came to naught."

Harklan nodded.

"Unfortunate. I allowed myself to hope that it would be possible, but I guess not."

Alaric shook his head.

"I am sorry. We tried for several decades to make it work but to no avail. However, that is not currently what concerns me. What concerns me most is how it came to be here. We very strictly control shipments of Quintessence. We mine only very small amounts at a time and those are shipped directly to an alchemist, within the Elder Hive in Transylvania, who makes the usable form for vampires. The fact that some of that has found its way somewhere else is of great concern."

Harklan nodded again, handing the paper back to Alaric.

"Could someone be using it as a recreational drug? They were shot up with a bunch of other stuff."

Alaric shook his head, accepting the paper and folding it neatly in half.

"No, especially not by a bearer of Cursed Blood. The Curse reacts badly to the introduction of Quintessence. It would likely be the farthest thing from pleasant. That's one of the reasons that…"

Alaric paused, his eyebrows furrowing. He unfolded the paper again and looked over it.

"Have you thought of something, Underlord?" Harklan asked, not sure he really wanted an answer.

Alaric stared silently at the page for several moments. Eventually, he looked up, folding the page and turning towards the door.

"I hope I have not, Harklan. I sincerely hope I have not. Please contact me immediately if any more of your Waifs transform again before the next full moon. Especially if their eyes begin to glow blue."

Harklan bowed slightly, opting not to answer out loud and risk further agitating the vampire.

Alaric nodded and then quickly left the room, leaving Harklan to breathe a quiet sigh of relief.

* * *

Angelica stood near the end of the table watching Alaric and Hivelord Andros studying several documents on the illuminated screens.

"Are you sure you wish me to be here, Hivelord?" She asked, her hands clamped tightly together behind her back.

The Hivelord nodded, moving one document to one side of his screen to look at another below it.

"Yes, Suite Lord. I do hope that we can resolve things peacefully, but I would like you to be here to try and help deter violence just the same."

Angelica nodded, adjusting her arms to try and keep her shoulders from growing tense. She watched Alaric reading over shipping and inventory documents with a grim expression she could remember seeing only a handful of times before. She shook herself, trying not to think about what dark omens that expression might foretell, and ensured she was standing at attention.

Almost an hour passed before the door beside Angelica opened and Overlord Burchard entered the room, wearing a freshly pressed black coat with red trim and buttons.

"You called for me, Hivelord?" Burchard noticed Angelica and nodded stiffly. "Suite Lord."

"Overlord." Angelica returned the nod, doing her best to sound respectful.

"Please take your seat, Burchard. Alaric and I have something that we must address with you."

Burchard made his way to his seat at the Hivelord's right hand and sat down. Alaric handed a folded paper to the Hivelord, who passed it across to Burchard.

"Look at this and tell me what it looks like to you, Burchard."

Burchard accepted the paper and unfolded it. Angelica noticed the Overlord immediately stiffen, though he tried to act otherwise.

"A chemical report. Several illicit substances, among other things."

The Hivelord nodded slowly.

"And what of the peaks that were not labeled?"

Burchard studied the page for a few more moments before placing it on the table.

"Possibly alchemical reagents, a few of these do seem familiar but I cannot place them in my memory. What is this report from?"

Alaric loosely folded his hands and placed them on the tabletop.

"These were blood samples from the two werewolves killed the night following the full moon. I have already had this test checked and have received word back from Master Faust in the Elder Hive. He confirmed that the unlabeled chemicals on this report are decaying alchemical silver and modified Quintessence."

Burchard's eyebrows rose in surprise.

"What possible use could a werewolf have for Quintessence?"

"That is not what our concern here is." Alaric stated.

Burchard's eyebrows now furrowed.

"What do you mean, Underlord?" Burchard placed subtle emphasis on Alaric's title.

Alaric chose not to respond and the Hivelord answered in his place.

"How did these werewolves find themselves in possession of Quintessence in the first place? Only our Hive has unrestricted access to it. What little of it we allow to leave is sent directly to Master Faust to be synthesized into Soleum Tempus."

Burchard frowned.

"That does seem concerning. Is it possible that a shipment did not reach Transylvania?"

Alaric shook his head, swiping a document across the table from his screen to Burchard's.

"Every shipment we sent to the Elder Hive arrived on schedule. They were signed for by Master Faust, who also verified the amounts shipped."

Burchard glanced over the list on his screen.

"If that is the case, is it possible that someone managed to smuggle some out from our stocks?"

Alaric swiped another document.

"We double-checked our inventory. There is a seven and one-quarter ounce discrepancy between what the miners reported bringing up and what we have on hand."

Burchard nodded, ignoring the inventory he had been sent.

"That sounds like you found the missing Quintessence then."

The Hivelord selected another document and slid it across to Burchard.

"Except that, despite not being taken out of the inventory, two shipments totaling seven and one-quarter ounces were signed out and shipped elsewhere. Do you know who signed for those shipments?"

Burchard stared down at the document, his fists clenched tightly on the table's surface.

"It was you, Overlord." Alaric ensured he put a, not so subtle, emphasis on Burchard's title.

Burchard frowned deeply.

"That doesn't mean anything. You can't claim I gave the werewolves Quintessence. They can't even use it."

Alaric nodded.

"Not under normal circumstances. However, the Quintessence found in the werewolves' blood had been modified through alchemy. Alongside alchemical silver and a host of Immunosuppressant drugs, it is clear this was being used to try and directly attack the werewolves' Cursed Blood and send them into a frenzy."

The Hivelord held up one hand to Alaric, who nodded and did not continue.

"Whatever it was or was not used for, the fact remains that Quintessence has left our Hive and did not go to the Elder Hive. This is an enormous breach in protocol. A breach that we cannot simply overlook. Where did the two shipments you signed for go, Burchard?"

Burchard growled.

"I cannot believe you would think that I would do anything to endanger this Hive. I have been the Overlord of this hive for over a hundred years. I have labored all that time to ensure that the Hive remained productive and safe." He waved at the documents in front of him. "And yet you would take this flimsy 'evidence' over my word?"

"Why?"

Burchard paused in his rant, remembering that Angelica was still present in the room.

"Why would you do this? To anyone who shares our Curse?" Angelica's eyes glistened.

"Angie, please." Alaric spoke softly, his expression pained.

Angelica shook her head, struggling to contain herself.

"He forced me… to take…"

Angelica gasped as she felt a hand close around her throat and press her up against the wall.

Burchard glared at Angelica, squeezing tightly to close off her airway.

"Remove your hand from my Blood-bonded."

Alaric stood just behind Burchard, no sound or stirring of the air betraying when he had moved. His voice was dangerously quiet and his hand was held like a knife, pointed at the back of Burchard's head. A subtle golden aura settled around his head and shoulders as his silver hair seemed to become weightless and took on an unearthly glow.

Angelica choked, trying to breathe, but there was a fiery glint in her eye and her hair started to glow and lift weightlessly into the air as well.

"That is enough."

A quiet voice resonated across the room with an air of absolute authority. Hivelord Andros stood slowly from his chair, his eyes nothing but glowing red orbs.

Angelica's hair returned to normal and settled around her face and shoulders. Burchard struggled but released Angelica and lowered his hand.

"Let him come to me, Alaric." The Hivelord's voice filled the room.

Alaric glanced over his shoulder and, after a few moments, his aura faded away. A few more seconds and his hair returned to normal as well and he lowered his hand with a nod.

"Stand before me, Burchard."

Burchard slowly turned and shuffled to the other end of the table and stood passively in front of the Hivelord.

Hivelord Andros's eyes continued to glow brightly, all trace of pupils and iris erased by the color of blood.

"Speak. Where did you send the shipments of Quintessence?"

"I was tasked to send them to an Elder's estate." Burchard spoke in a monotonous voice, as if drugged or hypnotized.

The Hivelord leaned closer.

"To which Elder did you send them?"

For a fleeting moment, Burchard struggled to resist.

"E-Elder Jayin."

The Hivelord stood straight again.

"Sleep, Burchard." He commanded.

Burchard's eyes closed and he collapsed onto the floor. The Hivelord's eyes faded back to normal, and he sat back in his seat.

Angelica gasped as air filled her lungs again, stumbling forward and being caught in Alaric's arms. Alaric supported her as she coughed for a few moments until she caught her breath again, then he lightly touched her bruised neck.

"Are you alright?" He asked her gently.

Angelica nodded carefully.

"Yes, My Love. I'm sorry, I could not stop myself from speaking." Her voice was hoarse and she tried to clear her throat.

Alaric carefully brushed her neck, his hand faintly glowing with golden power as he healed her bruises.

"Perhaps I should have expected this of Burchard." The Hivelord said from his seat. "I am sorry Angelica, Alaric. I should not have expected him to answer willingly. I apologize for his actions."

Angelica suddenly seemed to notice the Overlord lying on the ground.

"What happened?" She asked, her voice having returned to normal. "He was just in front of me."

Alaric brushed Angelica's hair back from her shoulders.

"Hivelord Andros is an Archlord-class vampire. I know you have not lived in Hives where that means much, so it is not surprising you have not experienced this before. Lesser vampires cannot resist the Hivelord's command if he so chooses. He commanded Overlord Burchard to sleep, and he will remain asleep until he is commanded to wake by another Archlord-class vampire."

Alaric smiled slightly at Angelica.

"You losing conscious thought for a moment is a side effect of the Hivelord's command."

Hivelord Andros bowed his head.

"I apologize, Angelica, I try to avoid using my abilities whenever possible. Though, perhaps in this instance, I should have used them sooner."

Angelica quickly shook her head.

"No, that's alright Hivelord. I was just confused for a moment, that's all. I don't think it is unreasonable to hope to avoid using force."

Angelica pursed her lips for a moment.

"I guess I'm not exactly the right person to be saying that."

The Hivelord chuckled, and Angelica felt her cheeks burn slightly.

Alaric smiled at her and carefully took hold of her chin, turning her face to one side.

"All types of people are needed. I wouldn't change you for the world." He planted a gentle kiss on the two white bite marks on her neck.

Angelica let out a grumpy sigh, certain now that her cheeks were bright red.

The Hivelord let the two have a moment and then spoke again.

"I will send Overlord Burchard to the Elder Hive. They may decide what to do with him there. What do you think we should do Alaric? Knowing now that Quintessence has left our Hive, and is being used for an unknown purpose."

Alaric turned to face the table, taking a moment to think.

"I think it would be best to contact the Enclave Archons and warn them to watch for unusual behavior among their charges. Also, perhaps it would not be unwise to investigate Elder Jayin's estate. Whether he was involved with what happened, or the Quintessence was merely stolen from him, we should try to track down where it is now. If we are lucky, we may find the rest of it before it can be distributed to unwitting individuals."

The Hivelord nodded a few times, thinking for a moment. Then the grin of an old man who is plotting something appeared on his face.

"Suite Lord Angelica, I would like to apologize for what happened to you this evening. Would you please be so kind as to allow me to give you a gift for your sacrifices?"

Angelica frowned, certain that she did not like the look on the Hivelord's face.

"It isn't necessary. I would never ask for anything in return for doing my duty. Though, I am certain you are not about to let me refuse."

The Hivelord continued to grin.

"Well if you would allow me, I wish to reward you for all your hard work. I know we are about eighty years late now, but how about I grant you a honeymoon trip to Europe?"

Angelica blinked in surprise and it was Alaric's turn to frown.

"Hivelord, I couldn't possibly leave right now. Especially after losing Overlord Burchard and..."

"It will be a wonderful trip, I am sure." The Hivelord ignored Alaric. "You can visit many tourist attractions. You could even visit some of our esteemed Elders in Europe, and maybe visit one of the largest Enclaves in the world too while you are there."

Alaric suddenly realized what the Hivelord was doing, as did Angelica.

"Now that you mention it, that does seem nice." She said, a smile starting to grow on her face. "And lately I haven't had nearly as much time to spend with My Love as I would like."

Alaric glanced over his shoulder at Angelica, and she smiled brightly at him. He shook his head with a sigh.

"I suppose if we can get ahead of schedule in the next couple of days, we could shut down operations and I could spare the time to travel a bit. If you are alright with running things alone while I am gone that is, Hivelord."

The Hivelord nodded, his grin growing wider.

"Excellent. I hear the south of France is lovely this time of year."

5

Chapter Five

Angelica sipped at her cup of tea, looking up at the Eiffel Tower which was brightly lit against the night sky.

"It was nice of Hivelord Andros to pay for a trip for us. Though, as much as I appreciate getting to see the Eiffel Tower, I feel like flying us to Paris is a bit farther away from the south of France than necessary."

Alaric sat across the small table, reading a magazine. He closed the magazine and placed it on the table, smoothing his black button-up shirt, and took a drink of water from a glass next to him.

"The Hivelord is trying to make it look like we really are on a honeymoon. He suggested the south of France because one of the current leaders of the Elder Council has her estate there."

Angelica nodded, taking a bite from a piece of toast, careful not to get any crumbs on her red frilled shirt.

"Is that Elder Amalia? I haven't met her before, I don't think. Of course, I don't believe I have been to France since..." She paused for a moment to think. "Goodness, probably since before the Revolution."

Alaric chuckled.

"It has been a while then, hasn't it? You must have been quite young the last time you were here."

Angelica pouted at Alaric.

"I was already in my nineties."

Alaric nodded, eating the last bite of his own toast with a smile on his face.

"Quite a young flower indeed then."

Angelica frowned and turned back to look at the city, determined not to let Alaric tease her into blushing.

"Well, when was the last time you were in France?"

Alaric took a moment to think, sipping at his water again.

"I believe I was here helping relocate some vampires to a new Hive when Francois the First decided to expand his hunting lodge."

Angelica giggled girlishly, glancing at Alaric out of the corner of her eye and placing one hand over her mouth.

"My, what an old man you are."

Alaric nodded in agreement.

"An unfortunate truth."

Angelica scoffed, trying not to actually laugh.

"So have you met Elder Amalia? What is she like?"

Alaric nodded again.

"I have met her on many occasions. If I had to describe her I would say she likes to act the part of an innocent, though she enjoys her schemes more than Hivelord Andros ever has. It also helps that she awakened her Cursed Blood very early, so she looks deceptively young."

Angelica took another bite of toast as she listened, answering after she swallowed.

"I heard she looked youthful, but is it really so much different than people like us? Neither one of us looks like we are older than our mid-twenties after all. Well, aside from your hair I suppose."

Alaric chuckled.

"Elder Amalia looks to be in her early teens. If she were here with us, it would probably not be too difficult to convince most passersby that she was our daughter."

Angelica blinked in surprise, somewhat stunned, trying to imagine such a person.

Alaric grinned and continued.

"Despite her looks, though, she is a first-generation vampire. Daughter of Elder Olbrecht, the first to be touched by the Origin Cursebearer. There are few, even among the Elders, who are as powerful as she is."

Angelica carefully lifted her cup and sipped her tea, deep in thought.

"Are we going to visit her estate? Like Hivelord Andros wants?"

Alaric nodded, leaning back in his chair.

"It would be wise to do so. We would like to visit Elder Jayin's estate as well. As he is also a member of the Elder Council, making the pretense of paying respects to other Elders first will make it less likely we will be turned away. Elder Amalia is among the better choices we have for that purpose."

Angelica looked down into her tea, seeing a distorted reflection of her face looking back at her.

"I was all for this idea initially, but it's starting to feel a little daunting."

Alaric smiled and watched her for a few moments, then held his hand out to her and rested it on the table.

Angelica looked at his hand for a few seconds, then set her tea cup down and reached out to hold it.

"We can't be in too much of a hurry. We still have to look like we are enjoying a late honeymoon."

Alaric leaned forward, lifting Angelica's hand to his lips and kissing it.

"Would you join me for a walk through the city before the sun rises?"

Angelica sighed, glancing around to see if anyone was around to stare at them.

"It would be rude of me to refuse, My Love."

Alaric stood and helped Angelica to her feet. They turned and made their way down a quiet lane that led towards the Eiffel Tower. Alaric put his arm around Angelica's waist and pulled her closer to him as they walked.

Angelica couldn't decide if she wanted to put her arm around Alaric or push him away, her eyes scanning the streets to see how many people might see them.

Alaric smiled and leaned closer to her.

"We are in Paris, the City of Love. No one will pay any heed to another couple wandering the streets." His lips brushed her ear as he spoke and she felt her cheeks immediately burning.

Angelica grumbled, putting her arm under his and around his back, resting her head on his shoulder to hide her face from him.

"You're enjoying this aren't you?"

"Should I not enjoy the company of the one I chose to Bond with?"

Angelica squeezed him, knowing she wouldn't be able to stop blushing if she looked at him directly.

"You know what I mean. You enjoy making me blush when other people are around."

Alaric chuckled, resting his head against hers.

"Of course. Everyone knows you as the fierce and reliable Suite Lord. I want them to see the cute and beautiful woman beneath the title as well."

Angelica paused, and Alaric stopped beside her. She waited for several seconds, then turned around and threw her arms around him.

"I really should bite you for that."

Alaric put his arms around her, pulling her even closer to him. He tilted his head to one side for her and, placing one hand on the back of her head, pressed her toward him lightly.

"If you wish to, I am all yours. Though we are still out in the open, aren't you worried about being seen?"

Angelica pouted, her cheeks burning again as she looked at Alaric's bite scars and remembered their Bonding ceremony. After a few minutes, she merely leaned forward and kissed his neck.

"I'll let you off easy this time." She said grumpily.

Alaric released her, taking a step back and leaning forward to place his forehead against hers.

"Then I look forward to the next time."

Angelica pulled back slightly and gently bumped her head against his, wondering if her cheeks could turn any more red.

"Be nice to me."

Alaric grinned and stepped away, holding his hand out to her again.

After a moment, Angelica reached out and laced her fingers with his and they started walking again.

"Shall I grant a wish for you then? Will you be happier if I do? Anything in my power, I will grant." Alaric spoke softly.

Angelica tilted her head to one side in thought, glad that the night air was cool.

"Hmm, I'm not sure. I am in Paris, with My Love. Is there anything I should want more than that?"

Alaric smiled.

"Can you think of nothing?"

Angelica looked up at him with a smirk.

"Perhaps I will simply save my wish for later. Perhaps I will use it to force you to cuddle with me on our long train ride tomorrow."

Alaric chuckled.

"That is acceptable." He said, lifting her hand and kissing it again. "Though you needn't use a wish for something I would already do if you asked."

Angelica felt her smirk turning into a smile and quickly pouted.

"Then I will think of something truly monumental for you to do on my behalf."

Alaric looked up into the sky, his eyes reflecting the numerous city lights.

"I look forward to it."

* * *

The maid, in a stereotypical French maid outfit, bowed deeply.

"We are honored to have Lords of one of our great Hives visit us."

Alaric and Angelica both nodded politely.

"We wished only to pay our respects to Elder Amalia while we were in France." Alaric spoke clearly, maintaining a straight-backed posture that Angelica tried to match.

The maid stood straight again, her hands clasped at her waist.

"I'm sorry, but our Lady Amalia has asked that she not be disturbed today. I apologize that you have traveled all this way for..." The maid twitched slightly, a red haze seeming to pass over her eyes.

After a few moments, the haze cleared and she nodded.

"Forgive me. Our Lady Amalia says she will see you, Lord Alaric. And you, Lord Angelica."

The maid bowed once again and waved towards the door.

"If you would be so kind as to follow me." She turned and stepped inside as she spoke, Alaric allowed Angelica to go first and then followed them both.

They made their way through a small entryway and then up a flight of stairs.

The top of the stairs opened up into a sitting room with a few chairs and a small end table. On the table was an oddly warped vase with a strange green-orange glaze. Opposite the stairs was a large set of double doors.

The maid led them to the doors and carefully opened them.

"My Lady, the guests you requested are here."

The maid waited for a moment and then stepped aside and waved Alaric and Angelica inside with another bow.

Angelica stepped inside to find it was a moderately sized dining room. Alaric joined her as the doors closed behind them. He turned and faced the head of the dining table and bowed.

"Elder Amalia. Honorable Greetings."

Angelica turned and bowed with Alaric, noticing a small girl in a fancy blood-red dress sitting at the head of the table.

"Honorable Greetings." Angelica said, following Alaric's example.

The small girl appeared as if she were only twelve or thirteen, and she had the blackest hair Angelica had ever seen. She sat quietly, looking down at them imperiously with her sharp golden eyes, but cracked after a few moments and smiled childishly.

"Lord Alaric, how many years has it been? I am surprised you have returned to Europe. Though, I am glad you have chosen to visit me."

Alaric stood upright and smiled politely.

"I believe it's been a little over a hundred and fifty years. Since the last time that the Great Plains Hive was asked to attend the Elder Council. I came to Europe because Hivelord Andros was gracious enough to give me the time to finally take a honeymoon trip."

Alaric motioned to Angelica, who bowed again.

"This is Suite Lord Angelica, my Blood-bonded."

The small girl nodded, continuing to smile, almost excitedly.

"I have heard of your exploits, Lord Angelica. If you have captured the heart of our Lord Alaric you must be truly exceptional. I am pleased to finally meet you in person."

Angelica shook her head, doing her best to remain calm so her cheeks would not turn red.

"I do my best to fulfill my duty, but I would not call myself exceptional. It is, however, an honor to finally get the opportunity to meet you in person, Elder."

The small girl grinned happily, revealing her sharp canine teeth.

"Would you join me for an evening meal?"

Alaric half bowed but shook his head.

"We could not ask to impose on you in such a way. We wished only to take this opportunity to pay our respects. Besides, we did not bring appropriate attire for such an event."

The small girl slipped from her chair and approached them.

"Nonsense. You hadn't planned to travel to West Germany to visit Elder Mihail until after tomorrow night. I must insist you stay for a meal."

Alaric shook his head with a sigh.

"I see Hivelord Andros has made our plans known."

The small girl grinned again.

"Come," She clapped twice and a butler quickly entered the room. "I will provide you with appropriate attire."

The small girl turned to the butler and waved at Alaric.

"Please take Lord Alaric and find him something suitable to wear for the evening meal. Have the cooks prepare food for two additional guests as well."

Alaric bowed, doing his best not to sigh again, and then followed the butler from the room.

After he left, the small girl grabbed Angelica's hand and pulled her the other way.

"Now just us girls can talk. I'll also find you a nice dress to wear for dinner."

Angelica was stunned by the small girl's strength and was dragged along for a few moments before she was able to get a hold of herself and follow willingly.

They hurried down a long hall and through a bright red door. The door led them into a bedroom, where the small girl let go of Angelica's hand and rushed over to a wide folding door. She pushed aside the door to reveal an enormous walk-in closet.

"Let's take a look. Let me know if you see anything you like." The small girl was practically bouncing.

Angelica blinked, surprised by the huge selection of expensive clothes and shoes lining the walls.

"I could never choose from such an exquisite collection, Elder."

The small girl pulled a black and red ball gown from the wall and held it up.

"Please, call me Amalia. What about this?"

Angelica grimaced a little.

"That feels like too much. I would prefer something simpler, El.. um, Lady Amalia."

Amalia grinned, putting the dress back.

"You don't need to be as stiff as Alaric, you know. I'm only an Elder when dealing with official Council business. I find that acting like that all the time dulls my senses."

She pulled down a short, black dress with spaghetti straps and a very deep V cut into the front that almost reached the waistline.

"What about this one? I'm sure Alaric would love to see you in it."

Angelica felt her cheeks burning.

"I would never be able to wear something like that in public."

Amalia giggled, putting the dress back and shuffling through some more.

"Suit yourself." She said, pausing a moment to look at another dress. She shook her head and continued her shuffling.

"You know, many years ago, I would have been jealous of you."

Angelica blinked in surprise.

"Jealous? Why would someone like you be jealous of me?"

Amalia turned her head to smile at Angelica, a far more mature smile than she had been using.

"Believe it or not, I once fancied Alaric myself."

Angelica got a nervous knot in the pit of her stomach. She realized she could feel, as the air in the room changed, that the person before her carried a very heavy presence. The unmistakable presence of an Elder Vampire.

"Perhaps there is some small part of me that still does. Though, even for one such as I, Alaric can feel unapproachable."

Amalia looked Angelica up and down, her smile lightening almost imperceptibly.

"Seeing you stand by his side allows me to see what it was he needed. Someone who was strong enough to stand with him proudly, without care for who and what he is. Nor concern for how truly special he is."

Amalia returned to her dress sorting.

"Not an old woman with the heart of a smitten young girl who could do nothing but ask to be doted on."

Angelica felt herself frown slightly.

"There is nothing wrong with wanting to be doted on a little."

Amalia laughed.

"What a unique woman you are. If it is you, perhaps I am not so sad to let him go."

She pulled out a black sundress with red trim and red lace frills that reached from the left shoulder down to the right hip.

"This one suits you I think."

Angelica nodded, just glad that it mostly covered everything.

"I suppose I could wear that."

Amalia grinned excitedly and pulled Angelica into the closet.

In a matter of minutes, Angelica found herself stripped down and already in the dress. It happened so quickly she hadn't even had the chance to feel properly embarrassed.

They returned to the dining room and found Alaric sitting at the table waiting for them.

Alaric stood as they entered, now wearing a blood-red suit and coat. He bowed to them and pulled out a chair for Angelica.

"You look radiant." He told her as she went to sit down.

Angelica did her best to ignore the compliment.

"And you look as sharp as I would have expected, My Love."

Alaric slid the chair in beneath her and then took the seat next to her.

"I would have preferred something more befitting my station."

Amalia sat in her chair at the head of the table, a playful grin on her face.

"Is it truly so much more red than what you normally wear?"

Alaric shook his head.

"Perhaps not much, but I only wear as much red as I do because Hivelord Andros insists on it. As Underlord, I should be wearing little more than the Suite Lords."

Amalia grinned, picking up a small bell and ringing it.

"You could wear the red if you so wished. You are not, by any means, a weak Lord. I judged as much long ago, and I stand by my decision."

Angelica glanced at Alaric and he nodded without her having to ask any questions.

"Elder Amalia has asked me before, on several occasions, to join the Elder Council."

Angelica felt her eyebrows rise and she looked back and forth between Alaric and Amalia.

"He, of course, refused my requests." Amalia said, pouting. "Even though I believe the Council would benefit greatly from his presence."

Alaric smiled politely as the double doors opened and a handful of maids wheeled in carts with dishes and covered food.

"I prefer to put my skills to work taking care of the Great Plains Hive and studying the Quintessence."

Amalia sighed as the maids began setting the table.

"I suppose you take after your father in that regard. I won't force you of course, but I do wish you would reconsider. I would even give Lord Angelica a position in the Elder Guard so she could accompany you."

Alaric chuckled, placing his hand on Angelica's.

"Much as I would enjoy seeing Angie in uniform, I must still decline. Especially now, since the Hive is short an Overlord."

Amalia raised her arms to allow a maid to place a handkerchief on her lap.

"Oh yes, I do recall Hivelord Andros said something about sending Overlord Burchard to the Council for punishment. Though he did not elaborate. What elicited such a response?"

Alaric frowned, sparing a glance at the maids in the room.

Amalia snapped her fingers and her eyes flashed red for a moment. The maids all twitched and froze in place, their eyes covered by a red haze.

"What has happened with my Hive?" Amalia's childish facade instantly fell away, her face now a serious mask of authority that would not have been out of place on a queen.

Alaric looked around and, despite the maids being frozen, waved one hand and caused all the doors into the room to shut tightly.

"The night after the full moon, two Waif class werewolves transformed and attacked an Aspect who has now been conducted into Master Koyane's care. Tests of the blood of both Waifs came back showing some amount of Quintessence in their blood. That, along with alchemical silver and a host of immunosuppressant drugs, leads us to believe it was used to attack their Cursed Blood and drive them into a frenzy that ended up transforming them. When we investigated, we found that several ounces of our stock of Quintessence had gone missing. That same amount was signed for, and sent outside the Hive, by Overlord Burchard. Not to the Elder Hive, but directly to the estate of Elder Jayin."

Amalia frowned deeply.

"What possible purpose could Jayin have for raw Quintessence? He can receive as much Soleum Tempus as he could need from the Elder Hive without question."

Alaric shook his head.

"I could not say. As a reagent for alchemy, it could have some use. For sorcery though, it is an unrivaled catalyst. Elder Jayin could not use it for that himself, but I imagine any number of sorcerers would do anything to get their hands on it. It also remains to be seen whether Elder Jayin was directly responsible for what happened, or if it was removed from his sphere of influence and was used by someone else."

Amalia nodded.

"I see. So you did not come here today to pay respect, but to make an excuse to investigate Elder Jayin."

Alaric nodded in return.

"We do pay our respects to you, Elder. There is no reason we would come here and not do so. But our purpose in making the entire trip was as a pretense so that we will be more welcome upon arriving to visit Elder Jayin."

Amalia sighed, an unpleasant look on her face.

"I will have to ensure that the matter of Burchard is put off for a time, to allow you your investigation before Jayin is made aware. If he is innocent, then your testimony shall clear him as soon as it is brought up in Council. Should he be found guilty, we will wish to restrain him as soon as he is accused so that he may not escape judgment."

Amalia looked up at Alaric and Angelica, frowning.

"I am sorry the two of you cannot properly spend your honeymoon together."

Angelica smiled back, though sadly.

"It's okay, we knew when we came that it wouldn't be a carefree trip. But we have, hopefully, many many more centuries together. There is no need for us to hurry. We will find time for each other. There are other things in the world far more important for us to worry about right now."

Alaric squeezed Angelica's hand.

"It is our responsibility to ensure that everyone has peace. When that peace is safe, perhaps we will find the time for a real honeymoon."

Amalia smiled, a wave of her hand unfreezing the maids, who continued working as if nothing had happened.

"Then I hope you will visit me again when that happens. I would so love to dress Lord Angelica in the most beautiful dresses again."

Angelica glanced at Alaric and blushed when he grinned.

"I would like to see that myself."

6

Chapter Six

"I see." Elder Mihail nodded carefully from behind his desk, his silver hair almost shining in the dim office light. "That does seem to bear an ill portent."

Alaric nodded in return.

"We haven't made Overlord Burchard's actions known yet, and Elder Amalia thinks it best that we do not until we have been able to gather more information."

Mihail nodded once again, carefully considering everything he had been told.

"I must concur. Whether we can truly attribute these actions to malice on Elder Jayin's part should be ascertained before we make any further decisions on the matter. I may, however, ask Hivelord Andros to send me the report you spoke of. I would very much like to ensure I know what to look out for in the unfortunate case that a similar event transpires here."

Alaric nodded again.

"That may be wise. We planned on visiting the London Enclave before making our way to Elder Jayin's estate so that we may warn the Pack Leader there to look out for any unusual behavior among his charges. I hope it will allow us to get ahead of any problems that may arise. Though, in the best case, we would like to find the rest of the Quintessence before it can be used for any nefarious purpose."

Mihail opened a drawer on his desk, pulling out a piece of decorated stationery.

"Allow me to write you a letter of introduction to Pack Leader Woodrow. He is an old man now, and wary of strangers, but he is intelligent and could still put down most of the charges in the Enclave if he felt so inclined."

Mihail took a pen and began writing.

"May I say, I am grateful you brought all of this to my attention."

Alaric shook his head.

"Not at all. We wanted you to be made aware of the situation. Elder Amalia also wished to have someone else on the council who would be prepared to stand with her as an impartial judge, regardless of what we discover. As one of the oldest members of the Elder Council and a current council leader, she considered you one of the best options available."

Mihail nodded, setting aside his pen.

"I am honored by Elder Amalia's trust in me." He folded the letter he had written and slipped it into an envelope. "Hopefully this is merely a misunderstanding, or an accident, and we will be able to judge Elder Jayin merely on the mistake of not running his experiments through the Elder Hive. So long as we can recover the rest of the Quintessence, that is. I dare not consider what may happen should even a small amount end up in the hands of a sorcerer who wishes to do anything less than savory."

Mihail turned and looked at Angelica, who had been sitting quietly beside Alaric during their entire meeting.

"I apologize that we were only able to discuss business, Lord Angelica. I do hope we will have occasion in the future to speak at length. Most of us in the Council have been curious about the one Lord Alaric chose to Bond with. It was most gratifying to meet you in person."

Angelica bowed her head.

"It was my honor to be here. There is no need to apologize. We already knew we would have little time for leisure, even though that was our excuse for being here."

Mihail nodded and held out the letter to Alaric.

"Once the issue with Overlord Burchard and Elder Jayin is resolved, we will search for another to fill the position of Overlord within the Great Plains Hive. Once that is established, I do hope you will accept an invitation to return for a proper stay in Europe. My estate is open to you, and I am certain Elder Amalia would extend the same invitation. And, of course, you are always welcome at the Elder Hive."

Alaric stood from his chair and accepted the letter with a bow.

"You are most generous. Once we can comfortably leave our Hive again, I am sure Angie will do her best to convince me to accept the offer."

Angelica stood, with a large smile on her face, and also bowed.

"We would be honored."

Mihail bowed his head to them in return.

"I hope to swiftly hear good tidings."

Alaric motioned for Angelica to lead the way and they left the office.

They quickly moved through the large house and out the front door, where Alaric opened the back door of the car they had arrived in.

Angelica slid into the seat and laid back with a groan. Alaric closed the door and walked around the car, getting in on the other side. He knocked on the screen that divided the back seat from the driver.

"To the train station, if you would."

The driver nodded and started the car, shifting into gear and pulling out of the driveway immediately.

"It's been so long since I have met with Elders, I forgot how heavy the air feels when they are around." Angelica said, trying not to sound like she was whining.

Alaric smiled, reaching over and rubbing her back and neck.

"It can be tiring when you are not accustomed to them." He said. "As I recall, you used to say the same thing about me."

Angelica closed her eyes and leaned herself against Alaric's hand.

"Well, you are Elder Age after all. You just always felt really hard to approach. It was almost intimidating to be around you."

Alaric chuckled, carefully moving his hand back and forth across her shoulders to find stiff muscles to massage.

"I am sorry that I was so disagreeable."

Angelica sighed, flinching slightly as Alaric found a knot in her neck and pressed on it.

"It's fine. I know now that you are just a big softy who likes to tease me."

Alaric worked on the knot he had found until it disappeared, then leaned over and gently kissed her cheek.

"I am sorry that I am still so disagreeable."

Angelica smiled, her cheeks turning pink.

"You can make it up to me by massaging my whole back on the train ride."

Alaric nodded and sat up straight, letting his hand fall to his side.

Angelica glanced at him out of one eye, her lips curling into a pout.

"That doesn't mean you have to stop right now."

Alaric laughed quietly and put his hand on her back again.

* * *

Alaric pressed the call button next to the front gate of the large stone complex. Angelica uncomfortably adjusted her dark sunglasses, resisting the urge to glare angrily at the sun.

"What business do you have here?" A voice crackled through a speaker beside them.

"We were asked to visit. We have a letter of introduction from Elder Mihail of the Elder Council."

There were a few moments of silence before a door nearby opened and a young man with blonde hair stepped out.

"You vamps?"

Alaric nodded, pulling the envelope he had received from Elder Mihail out of his jacket pocket. He held it out to the young man.

"Indeed, we are. We have something important to discuss with Pack Leader Woodrow if he can spare a few minutes of time for us. I understand he may be busy and, if that is the case, we can return another time. Though this letter of introduction should at least explain who we are."

The young man took the envelope and looked at both sides.

"Yeah, alright. Gimme a minute and I'll go ask."

The young man turned and walked back through the door, closing it behind him.

"Abrasive young kid. Gives me the urge to smack him." Angelica grumbled.

Alaric chuckled quietly, reaching out and giving her hand a squeeze.

"Let us try our best to be respectful. The werewolves here are much more wary than the ones in the Central U.S. Enclave."

Angelica frowned.

"I know that." She grumbled a bit more and then frowned. "I'm sorry, My Love, the sunlight is annoying."

Alaric grinned, glancing at her from the side of his own dark sunglasses.

"I understand. We will be inside soon, whether here or at our hotel. We were unfortunate to visit England during an unprecedented sunny spell."

Angelica nodded, glancing around to see if there was any shade to stand in.

"It's probably because I'm here. I think the sun hates me."

Alaric laughed.

"You aren't exactly wrong, Angie. The sun hates all of us. It's a big angry ball of fire, after all." He nudged Angelica slightly. "Kind of like you."

Angelica pouted at him.

"I'm not angry."

"How generous of you."

Angelica frowned deeply, thinking about whether or not she should decide to be angry.

The large main gate clicked and swung open with a rusty squeal, the nearby speaker crackling to life.

"Straight down the main walkway. Woodrow's office is the last door on your left."

Alaric nodded to the speaker and took hold of Angelica's hand.

"Thank you, kindly."

Alaric led Angelica away before she could complain about the speaker being rude, following the instructions they had been given.

When they approached the end of the lane, they stopped in front of the last door and Alaric knocked lightly. There was a muffled reply from inside and Alaric turned the handle and opened the door.

Angelica stepped inside and Alaric closed the door behind them. They were in a large, sparsely decorated, office with a handful of filing cabinets and a large oak desk. Behind this desk sat a large older man with pure white hair and long bushy sideburns.

The large man leaned back in his chair and crossed his large arms over his equally large chest.

"I hear you are a Lord from an important Hive in America. That seems like an awful long way to travel for a visit just to exchange pleasantries. So what brings vampires to my Enclave so soon after the full moon?"

Alaric bowed, and Angelica followed suit.

"I do apologize for taking up your time. While we did wish to visit merely to see one of the largest and most well-respected Enclaves, we also have unfortunate news we thought important to share with you. I don't know if Elder Mihail mentioned it in his letter, but it is a sensitive issue we would wish you to keep confidential."

The large man nodded and stood from his desk. He walked around and stood in front of his two visitors.

"He did. But before we get to that, proper introductions. I am Pack Leader Woodrow Burton."

The large man held his hand out to Alaric.

Alaric accepted the handshake with a nod.

"I am Underlord Alaric, of the Great Plains Hive." Alaric motioned to Angelica with his free hand. "This is Suite Lord Angelica, my Blood-bonded."

Woodrow shook Alaric's hand firmly and was mildly surprised when Angelica reached out as well. He accepted her handshake, one side of his mouth tugging into some semblance of a smile.

"You don't carry yourselves as stiffly as other vampires."

Alaric smiled politely.

"I try to avoid getting caught up in the politics of the Elders and Hivelords. My concern is the well being of everyone else. Curse-Bloods and Pure-Bloods alike. Something often overlooked by those who look only at the big picture."

Woodrow smirked, some amount of bitterness showing in his expression. He walked back to his desk, turning and sitting on the polished wood surface which creaked from his weight.

"Now, what brought you to my Enclave?" He asked, crossing his arms again. "You said it was important, didn't you?"

Alaric nodded, his smile fading away.

"Have you heard of an incident, in an American Enclave, where two Waifs were killed?"

Woodrow nodded.

"Pack Leader Harklan sent a memo out to every Enclave stating that something had happened to that effect. He also said we should be vigilant in watching for suspicious behavior among our charges. Does that have something to do with what you came here for?"

Alaric nodded again.

"Indeed. It was not merely an accident. The two Waifs were given a drug that we believe was designed to attack their Cursed Blood. It sent them into a frenzy and they transformed... the night after the full moon."

Woodrow's lips parted slightly in surprise, and he slowly unfolded his arms.

"After? Waif class werewolves can't transform outside of a full moon."

Alaric shook his head sadly.

"Not only did they transform, they were drugged to the point that they were so far gone they would not respond to pain or force like normal. In the end, they died because the force needed to subdue them was far greater than they could bear. We were only lucky there were several Lord class vampires who had spent the day nearby and were able to stop them."

Woodrow scowled deeply.

"Is there more of this drug around? Do I now need to worry about my charges going on a rampage during any time of the day or night?"

Alaric sighed and shook his head.

"Unfortunately, we simply do not know. It requires a very rare ingredient to make. One that we vampires usually control very strictly. However, one of our own allowed a small amount to be taken. It isn't so much that we need to worry about it becoming widespread, but if all of it was converted into this drug, there could be several dozen doses. With that much, deaths would become almost inevitable. I'm sure you can understand how many hundreds of years of work that could cause to be undone."

Woodrow growled.

"Yeah, we don't need people gettin' scared of us again. Even as is, we still occasionally have a problem. Is there some way we can fight the drug?"

Alaric thought quietly for a few moments.

"Nothing that would be particularly effective to a transformed werewolf. We could potentially filter it from their blood, but I doubt any hospital would take such a patient. The drug should take a few moments to take effect, and their eyes should glow blue. So our best bet would be to notice the drug taking effect and immediately isolate them. Beyond that, the most likely scenario would be keeping people on alert and, if any werewolves change, set traps and use other werewolves or vampires to lure them into the traps."

Woodrow shook his head.

"An enormous amount of trouble it sounds like."

Alaric scratched his chin.

"We could probably narrow down the number of individuals that would need to be watched. As I said, the two that transformed before also had other illicit drugs in their system. Most likely they were given the drug and told it was recreational. So your highest risks will probably be those most likely to search out drugs and use them."

Woodrow nodded, standing up and walking around behind his desk.

"Well, that's a start at least. I will have some of my Alphas start working on something to trap anyone who transforms, and I will contact some authorities to get permission to set the traps."

He glanced up as he sat down in his seat.

"While keeping the reason discreet, of course."

Alaric bowed.

"That would be appreciated. We did not come to Europe just to warn you. We hope to find the missing ingredients and the one responsible for making the drug. If we are lucky, all of my warnings will prove unnecessary."

"Never been lucky a day in my life." Woodrow complained as he grabbed a pen and a blank piece of paper. "I have to assume all of those drugs ended up in my Enclave."

Alaric nodded, a sympathetic smile appearing on his face.

"I understand. And if we do get lucky, perhaps having a few traps already set up for emergencies would not be an unwelcome addition to our full moon defenses."

Woodrow glanced up from his scribbling.

"That's not too bad, vampire. Not too bad."

Alaric smiled.

"I try to be as efficient as I can be. Anything that makes all of our lives easier and simpler is worth consideration. Avoiding future deaths by being able to contain escaped werewolves, instead of subduing them, would also be a positive. I've been considering ways to implement a similar system in the United States in recent months."

Alaric paused as Angelica tugged lightly on his sleeve. She held out her phone and pointed at the time.

"Oh dear, that late already? My apologies, Pack Leader, it seems we must be going. We will leave you to your work. It was an honor to meet you."

Angelica bowed slightly after putting her phone back in her pocket.

"It was an honor."

Woodrow nodded.

"The honor was mine. You should speak up more though, girl. I rarely meet a woman in your position strong enough to command attention. You don't need to stand passively behind your husband."

Angelica grinned brightly.

"Oh no, I just hate trying to explain complicated stuff. Especially important stuff. Alaric is good for that, so I let him do all the boring talking."

Woodrow laughed loudly, almost barking.

"I knew I liked you. You had a firm handshake too. You are welcome in my Enclave any time."

Angelica nodded with a smile.

"Thank you. If I ever get the chance to visit again, I shall. Hopefully with something less boring to talk about."

Woodrow grinned, bearing his perfect white teeth.

"I look forward to it."

Alaric chuckled, placing his hand in the small of Angelica's back and waving her towards the door.

"We will take our leave then. I wish you the best, Pack Leader Woodrow. If anything does happen, please do not hesitate to call on us. We will provide any and all support we are able."

Woodrow returned to his writing.

"Your Elder Mihail expressed the same. I appreciate the offer of support. Pray it is not needed."

Alaric nodded once, following Angelica through the office door.

"With all hope."

They closed the door behind them and turned towards the main gate.

"I think you made a new friend." Alaric said with a smile, nudging Angelica gently with his arm.

Angelica pouted.

"What do you mean? Pack Leader Woodrow seems like a good man. Besides, you say that like I don't have any friends at all."

Alaric grinned.

"Your Suite doesn't count."

Angelica now frowned.

"Why not? They are fun to talk to and hang out with. You said so yourself."

Alaric shook his head.

"They are completely enamored with you. That's hardly fair."

Angelica glared at Alaric as they waited for a moment for the front gate to open, then they stepped out and turned to walk down the street.

Alaric watched Angelica for a few minutes as they walked, eventually reaching out and gently lifting a lock of her hair.

Angelica glanced at him with a look akin to suspicion.

"What? Do I have something in my hair?"

Alaric smiled, carefully caressing her hair with his thumb.

"I don't believe so. It is soft and lovely to look at though."

Angelica's cheeks turned red and she tugged her hair out of his hand.

"Well then why do you need to touch it?"

Alaric chuckled, reaching out and taking her hand instead.

"Because I am also enamored with you."

Angelica grumbled, tightly squeezing his hand as they reached a corner and stopped to hail a taxi.

"That's hardly fair." She said, trying to think of some way to get back at him.

7

Chapter Seven

"Elder Jayin regrets that he was unable to be here to greet you himself. He was called away for Council unexpectedly."

The butler bowed. His eyes, sunken and dark, pointed firmly at the ground.

"The Elder, however, invites you to stay for the evening meal as an apology for being unable to entertain you himself."

Alaric nodded, a look of mild disappointment on his face.

"That is, indeed, unfortunate. We had no other plans for our evening meal. If we would not be imposing overmuch, we will accept the Elder's gracious invitation."

The butler stood up straight, though his eyes remained firmly pinned to the ground. He waved towards the door.

"Please, follow me."

Alaric, outside his usual habits, took the lead and followed the butler inside. Angelica followed closely behind, trying to make herself appear as small as she could.

They entered the dimly lit main hall and looked around. Despite the humidity outside, the air inside was dry and seemed to carry an oppressive weight.

The butler led them down a few corridors, then through a door. He held the door open for them, waving them towards a small dining table.

Alaric nodded, thanking the man before pulling out a chair for Angelica. Angelica sat and Alaric pushed her chair in for her before walking around the table and taking the seat across from her.

"The meal will be served in a moment. We appreciate your patience as we plate your food fresh." The butler spoke, more out of habit than to his guests, before turning and closing the door as he left.

"I don't like it here." Angelica whispered, once she was sure they were alone.

Alaric nodded carefully, his sharp eyes scanning the small dining room.

"Elder Jayin is rumored to be very demanding of those under his direct control. I've even heard rumors that he will often use his ability to Command lesser vampires, even when he could simply give a normal order and it would be followed. I saw only a small number of other servants, but each flinched away when they saw us coming."

Angelica frowned, an unhappy feeling settling in the pit of her stomach.

After several minutes of silence, the door they had entered through opened and a petite maid, with dark hair tied tightly in a bun with a pin and a piece of decorative lace, pushed a cart with two covered plates into the room. She carefully closed the door behind her and made her way over to the table.

She carefully placed the first plate in front of Angelica, then carried the second around the table and set it in front of Alaric.

"Is there anything you would like to drink with your meal?" The maid asked. Her voice was shaky, and it was apparent that she was straining to speak clearly.

Alaric spared a glance at the maid and then nodded to Angelica.

"I'll have a cup of tea. He would like just a simple glass of water." Angelica motioned to Alaric as she spoke.

The maid bowed, the lace decoration that was tied around her tightly twisted bun falling off her head onto the table.

Alaric gently picked up the decoration and held it out to her with a warm smile.

The maid gasped and shakily took it out of his hand.

"Please forgive my clumsiness." She sounded like she was going to start crying, but she quickly bowed again and rushed to take the cart back out of the room.

Angelica felt her heart aching for the poor maid and was starting to feel disdain for the master of the house.

"Are you sure you didn't want to ask for something else to drink?" She asked, trying to focus on Alaric instead of things that would make her more upset.

"I didn't think it wise for me to speak." He said, watching the door. "They know I am a Lord of some standing. They were likely instructed to treat us with the highest respect. You are much more personable than me and I would rather not add more stress than they probably already feel."

Alaric smiled sadly at Angelica for a moment when he noticed her frowning.

"I understand how you feel. Try to bear with it if you can."

Angelica nodded, shaking herself and trying to wipe the frown off her face.

They waited for a few more minutes until the maid returned, balancing a tray with a teacup and a glass filled with water.

She placed the tray on the table and took the teacup, setting it in front of Angelica. She did her best to smile and then reached for the tray that still had the glass of water on it. She took a sharp breath of surprise as Angelica grabbed her wrist.

"Are you okay? You try to smile, but I can see you crying beneath it. What's wrong?" Angelica looked up at the maid, genuine concern coloring her voice.

The maid's mouth moved a few times, her false smile quickly disappearing and tears welling up in her eyes.

Angelica quickly stood and wrapped her arms around the maid, hugging her tightly against her chest.

Alaric immediately heard the sound of weak, muffled sobs and quickly stood. He made his way around the table and peeked out of the door. Seeing no one, he carefully closed the door, ensuring the latch clicked shut before returning to his seat, sparing a glance at the drinks as he went.

"There, there little one," Angelica spoke softly. "it's okay. You are safe here. Let out the tears."

Alaric watched Angelica support the maid as she cried, but carefully reached across the table and took Angelica's tea cup. He held it near his nose and smelled it, a faint sour metallic scent entering his nostrils. He shook his head slowly as he set it aside, out of Angelica's reach.

They waited for several more minutes until the maid stopped shaking and then Alaric finally spoke.

"Are you well now?"

The maid stiffened at the sound of Alaric's voice. She nodded carefully but kept her face buried against Angelica's chest.

"That is good to hear. I am glad. I want to ask you some questions. You need not answer out loud, just nod or shake your head. I promise neither of us will hurt you, no matter your answers. Is that alright?"

After a few moments, the maid nodded.

"Were you forced to poison our drinks?"

The maid clenched her hands tightly.

Angelica placed a hand on the maid's head and carefully patted her hair.

"It's okay, I promise he won't do anything to you." She whispered.

Eventually, the maid slowly nodded.

"Did Elder Jayin invite us to this meal as an apology for being absent?"

The maid shook her head.

"Was he the one who told you to poison us?"

The maid started shaking again, but she nodded.

"Has he been doing anything the Council would not approve of?"

The maid hesitated for a moment but, eventually, she nodded her head. Angelica spared Alaric a glance and she could almost see the wheels in his head turning.

"Would you like to leave this place?"

The maid froze again. This time, after a few moments, she turned her head slightly to peek at Alaric. Alaric waited patiently for an answer, his eyes sharp but his expression gentle.

After several more moments, the maid hesitantly nodded her head.

Alaric nodded in return.

"Then I want to ask one more question. Before I do, I want you to know that no matter your answer we will still take you with us when we leave. We will send you to Elder Mihail's estate, where you may stay or be taken to an estate or Hive of your own choosing. I will not ask you to put too great a burden on yourself. Is that acceptable?"

The maid nodded.

"Would you be able to show me where Elder Jayin has hidden what he was working on?"

The maid absently grasped the front of Angelica's shirt and, after a moment, shakily nodded.

* * *

Alaric stood in front of an old desk and skimmed over several pages of notes, shuffling through them quickly.

Angelica stood nearby, her hands resting supportively on the shoulders of the maid who had led them to the basement of the estate.

Alaric set the notes aside, noticing a loose brick in the wall behind the desk. He carefully pried it free and pulled it out, revealing a compartment that held a frosted glass container.

Alaric pulled the glass container out of the compartment and opened it, revealing several ethereal blue crystals.

"This is most of the missing Quintessence." He said, carefully weighing the container in his hand. "Though, there is still some unaccounted for. If it was made into the drug, there are probably another six doses we haven't seen used yet." Alaric closed the container and placed it on the desk.

"Do you think it is here? Or do you think he took it somewhere else?" Angelica asked, patting the maid gently when she flinched.

Alaric shook his head.

"I don't believe it is here. Since Elder Jayin knew we were coming, he most likely sent it somewhere else. It is also possible he took it with him when he left so we wouldn't be able to find anything incriminating if his plan to poison us failed."

The maid hung her head and Angelica rubbed her shoulders gently.

"It's okay. You aren't at fault." Angelica said quietly.

Alaric stirred through some more papers, gathering a few into a neat stack. He placed the glass container on the stack and then held his hand over it.

A golden glow enveloped Alaric's hand and the stack of paper seemed to turn to liquid, wrapping itself tightly around the container. As the golden glow faded away, the liquid paper solidified into a single, seamless sheet.

Alaric lifted the new package and carried it over to the maid and held it out to her. The maid stared at the package, unsure what was expected of her.

Alaric smiled.

"I want you to carry this with you. No one will be able to take it from you, and only Elder Mihail will be able to open it. Take it with you to Elder Mihail's estate."

The maid carefully reached out, took the package, and nodded.

Alaric looked around the room.

"I am not sure there is much else we can glean from this place. We will have to use what evidence we have to accuse Elder Jayin."

Angelica nodded and Alaric turned to lead the way out of the basement. But, as he turned, he felt something catch his sleeve. He looked down and saw that the maid was pinching his sleeve between her thumb and pointer finger.

Alaric read the maid's face and carefully got down on one knee, looking up into her eyes.

"What is wrong? Is there something more you had wished to say?"

The maid nodded, working up the courage to speak.

"H-he... h-he wants to... break the... the Pact."

Angelica tilted her head to one side, not immediately understanding. Then she noticed Alaric's expression had turned dour, a frown growing on her own face as she started to realize what the maid had said.

Alaric gently reached up and held the maid's face in his hands.

"Are you certain, little one? I need you to be one hundred percent certain."

The maid nodded, tears filling her eyes again.

"H-he spoke... with someone... about it. Several times. He said... he said our kind should... should be free. H-he held us, b-but most of us could... could still hear."

Alaric nodded and gently patted the maid's cheek.

"Well done, little one. Thank you for telling me."

Alaric stood and turned away from the stairs that led back out of the basement. He looked around and selected a blank section of the wall.

"Angie, I need you to take her back to our hotel room. Arrange for her to be taken to Elder Mihail's estate. Then I need you to return to the London Enclave and warn Pack Leader Woodrow that there could be six more doses of the drug and to remain vigilant."

Angelica nodded.

"What are you going to do?"

Alaric shook his head.

"It is best if you do not know. Please take care of her. She is an important witness now. I am now certain that we must put a stop to what Elder Jayin plans."

Angelica nodded again.

"Alright. I will do my part. Be safe, My Love."

Alaric looked over his shoulder at her.

"And you as well. I will hurry to return to you."

Angelica nodded one more time, then gently turned the maid and led her up the stairs.

Alaric waited for several moments until he heard the door at the top of the stairs click shut. He then turned and faced the blank wall he had selected before and raised his arms, palms turned upward.

A dense golden aura settled around him as he began speaking a spell. His power raced through him and swirled into the room, scattering loose papers around his feet and across the room. He continued speaking, for several minutes, until his blue eyes began to glow gold.

"To the wilds, conduct me. Before the King and Queen, allow my knee to bend." Alaric's voice reverberated across the room and the blank wall began to change.

Glowing, golden vines began creeping up the wall, forming an archway that reached up to the ceiling. As the archway was completed, the bricks at the center began falling away, folding in on themselves and disappearing, leaving nothingness in its place.

A light appeared at the center of the black expanse that was left behind and, after a moment, it rushed forward and filled the archway with brightness equal to the noonday sun.

Another few moments went by and the bright light gradually faded away to reveal a small forest clearing.

Alaric lowered his arms, his golden aura fading away, and walked through the archway onto the clean grass of the clearing. The archway behind him began to fade and the brick wall quickly rebuilt itself.

In a matter of seconds, the basement room had returned to normal. A few scattered papers were the only indication that anything at all had changed.

8

Chapter Eight

Angelica walked along the street, doing her best not to glare at the last sliver of the setting sun that hadn't yet fallen below the horizon. She adjusted her dark sunglasses as she turned the corner and the Enclave gate came into view.

She approached the gate and pressed the call button near the speaker.

"The Enclave is currently closed. We aren't accepting visitors for the rest of the evening."

The man who answered was clearly annoyed.

Angelica did her best not to growl and took a deep breath before responding.

"Please just tell Pack Leader Woodrow that the vampire Angelica is here to speak to him. It is a matter of great importance, pertaining to what we discussed with him previously. Even if you don't want to let me in, please just ask Pack Leader Woodrow to come to the gate for just a moment."

There were several moments of silence before an answer came.

"Fine. If it will make you go away, I'll go ask. Then the Pack Leader can tell you to leave himself."

The man spoke with something like exasperation.

Angelica sighed.

"Thank you."

There was no response and Angelica assumed the man had already left.

Several minutes passed by, long enough for the sunset to begin fading and give way to true evening. Angelica took her dark sunglasses off and slipped them into one of her coat pockets.

Eventually, she saw someone approaching the gate from the main compound. She frowned as she realized it wasn't Pack Leader Woodrow, but the young man who had been watching the gate during their previous visit.

The young man walked up to the gate, clearly unhappy, and manually released the lock. He pulled the gate open enough for Angelica to enter and waved vaguely in the direction he had come from.

"Pack Leader says you can come in. Try to make it quick. I can't go home until we've locked up for the night."

Angelica fought to try and keep her frown from turning into a scowl.

"I will do my best to finish quickly, but I assure you this matter is of the utmost importance for your Enclave. If I was permitted to tell you what it was, I am sure you would rather stay a few minutes late to ensure it was taken care of."

The young man shook his head but, to Angelica's relief, he chose not to respond.

Angelica nodded politely and then hurried down the lane into the compound before the urge to say something nasty to the young man got any stronger. She moved quickly, counting the doorways she passed, until she reached the Pack Leader's office.

Angelica knocked at the door, waited a few moments for a response, then opened the door and stepped inside.

Pack Leader Woodrow was sitting at his desk with an open file folder, carefully reading over a document.

"I'm surprised you came back so quickly. Is your husband not with you this time?"

Angelica shook her head.

"No, Alaric had something important that urgently needed to be taken care of. I came to let you know we found most of the missing materials we were looking for."

Woodrow glanced up from his file.

"Most?"

Angelica nodded, a frown growing on her face again.

"Some of it is still missing. Alaric estimated that, if all of it was already turned into the drug, there are probably six more doses that we haven't witnessed being used yet. Until we find the rest of the missing materials, we should assume that is the number of possible transformations that could cause a problem before the next full moon."

Woodrow laced his fingers together.

"I see. Thank you for letting me know. Preparing for six werewolf attacks will be much simpler than trying to plan for dozens. We also won't need to implement nearly as many traps. I will still have to thank your husband for that idea though. I think it will take a great deal of stress off of us all during the full moon if capturing an escaped Waif or Alpha becomes necessary. Regardless of if we need them before then or not."

Angelica smiled and shook her head.

"Alaric spends a lot of time trying to think of ways to make full moons safer for everyone involved. That is one of the reasons he started negotiations with The Academy. He is hoping to release some of the tension of those nights. He is also hoping that, at some point, gathering and locking up werewolves on each full moon will become unnecessary."

Woodrow chuckled, leaning back in his chair.

"That would be nice. Though, I doubt it will happen in my lifetime. Sometimes I envy the long lives of you vampires." Woodrow grinned. "And then I remember that such a long life can be a curse all its own."

Angelica laughed.

"I know what you mean, but it is not so bad if you have someone to share it with. The years since my Bonding have been relatively short, but they have felt far more fulfilling than all my other years combined."

Woodrow's grin widened, and he nodded.

"Curious as I am, I won't be so ill-mannered as to ask you your age." Angelica grinned back.

"Old enough to be your great-great-grandmother, at the least.

A knock at the door interrupted their conversation.

"Come in." Woodrow called.

The door opened and the young man stepped into the room. He looked over at Angelica with a scowl.

"Are you done talking yet?"

Angelica frowned, but Woodrow huffed before she could say anything.

"Don't be disrespectful, Jack. She'll take as long as she needs to. Just go home if you're in such a hurry. I'll lock up the gate myself when she is done."

The young man named Jack grumbled and reached into his pocket.

"I was hoping she would just say her piece and leave." He pulled out a capped vial and ripped off the cap, revealing a needle. "But I am tired of waiting."

"Put that down." Angelica growled, half turning to face him, her hair taking on a fiery glow and floating off her shoulders.

"What are you doing, Jack? That better not be what I think it is." Woodrow stood from his chair as he spoke.

"Or what? Pack Leader." The young man spoke the title with disdain, jamming the needle into his leg.

Angelica was behind the young man in a flash, yanking the vial from his hand. She glared at the empty vial and tossed it aside.

"You fool. What are you doing?"

The young man turned and shoved Angelica, but her feet were firmly planted on the floor and he only managed to push himself backwards. He stumbled back and growled, sounding more animal than man as his eyes began to take on a blue glow.

"I'm no fool. I was just supposed to kill the Pack Leader, but now I'll just have to kill you both."

The young man's body started to twist and distort, his limbs stretching and pulling and growing longer. His clothes grew tight and then tore as his body swelled in size and thick brown fur burst through his skin. He threw his head back and a scream escaped his mouth that quickly became a loud howl as his nose and jaw pulled away from his face, with an unpleasant crunching sound, and quickly became a long muzzle.

The werewolf, now nearly nine feet tall, bared his teeth with a menacing growl. Saliva dripped from his mouth and his brightly glowing blue eyes held a crazed stare, trained on Angelica.

Angelica growled and raised her fists to fight. But, as the werewolf lurched forward, another werewolf tackled the first and they rolled across the office into the far wall.

This second werewolf was head and shoulders taller than the first and had pure white hair.

The white werewolf tore at the brown one with its claws, biting into its shoulder and throwing it across the office.

The brown werewolf landed on the desk, crushing it to splinters, and quickly rolled to its feet. It took a couple of running steps and dove into the white werewolf, knocking it off its feet and slamming it into the wall. The two werewolves clawed at each other, each trying to get their jaws around the other's throat.

A burst of fire lit the room as Angelica drove a kick into the head of the brown werewolf. In a split second, as the werewolf recoiled from the blow, she raised her left hand, grabbed it by the nape of its neck, and lifted it off of the ground. She turned and threw it, spinning and striking it in the air with her right hand, another burst of fire propelling it across the office into the opposite wall.

"Hold him down, Woodrow!" Angelica yelled. "I need to get my teeth into him if we don't want to end up killing him!"

"Better make it quick, kid is tough and I'm getting too old for this kind of tripe." The white werewolf spoke with a guttural semblance of Woodrow's voice.

Woodrow howled and pounced on the brown werewolf as he was trying to get back up. He locked his teeth onto the other werewolf's shoulder and twisted, throwing him into the center of the room and landing on top of him. Woodrow's immense weight pinned one of the brown werewolf's arms to his side, and one of his hands grappled with the free one.

Angelica rushed to Woodrow's side, sliding and driving one knee into the head of the other werewolf. She twisted and grabbed the brown werewolf's lower jaw, forcing his head back. She opened her mouth wide, feeling the powerful muscles in the roof of her mouth forcing her fangs to bear, making them longer.

With little hesitation she leaned down and forced her fangs into the werewolf's neck, feeling them pierce through his thick skin. Then, as blood flowed and she tried to separate the drug from it, memories rushed into her.

* * *

"So, can you do it?" Elder Jayin spoke, a disgusted frown on his face. "I know you are discontent with the Pack Leader's ways, but are you capable of killing him? Or of taking a life at all?"

Angelica felt her right hand thump against her chest and then heard Jack's voice respond.

"Of course I am. The Enclave needs to change. We shouldn't be the ones hiding away. If the Humans are scared of us, they can lock themselves up."

Elder Jayin's frown turned into a sneer.

"Excellent. I'm glad at least one of your kind understands we shouldn't be hiding like scared children."

Elder Jayin reached into the sleeve of his red council robe and pulled out a capped vial. He held it out and Angelica reached out and accepted it.

"This injection will allow you to transform outside of the full moon and make you stronger. I suggest you pick your time carefully. Woodrow has advanced in age, but he is a cunning old wolf. If you don't take him by surprise, when there is no one near enough to help him, he might still kill you."

Angelica felt bitter disdain rising in her heart, and she heard Jack speak again.

"I am not as weak as the Waifs. The Pack Leader may be an Archon but, with this medicine, even an Alpha like me could kill him."

Elder Jayin turned and faced away, clasping his hands behind him in the small of his back.

"Good. Then I will await the news of the 'tragic' death of the London Enclave's Pack Leader."

Angelica bowed and turned, making her way toward the door that would lead toward her destiny.

* * *

Angelica sat up straight, swishing a bitter liquid around her mouth. She turned and spit a pale blue liquid out, over her shoulder, onto the floor.

"I got most of it out. I drained a bit of blood too, so he should change back and stay passed out for a while."

Angelica made a face and spit again before wiping some blood off her chin.

Woodrow let go of the other werewolf and stood, striding over to his broken desk on all fours.

"Good, glad that's over with. I'm getting too old to be wrestling with upstarts who think they're tough stuff."

A snarl escaped between Woodrow's teeth as he swiped the remains of his desk to one side and grabbed a couple of large beach towels from under the mess. He turned and tossed one over the brown werewolf's lower half, then stood upright and held the second around his waist.

With a shudder, he shrank in size and his white fur receded until he looked like a normal human being once again. He adjusted his towel and tied it tightly around his waist.

"Always a pain getting new clothes after a transformation like that." Woodrow said, opening a small sliding panel behind where his desk had been. "I liked those pants too. Darn comfortable."

Woodrow reached into the open panel and pressed a button. Angelica heard a faint ringing sound somewhere else in the compound.

"Glad you swung by though. I probably would have had to kill the kid if I had been here by myself. Misguided idiot that he is, he is still one of my charges and I'm supposed to protect him."

Angelica rose to her feet, taking a moment to gather some more saliva and spit again.

"I was happy to help, though I should have taken the vial from him sooner. I'm just glad I was able to get the drug out of his system. Tastes disgusting though. Don't suppose you've got something to drink in here? Something strong, preferably."

Woodrow laughed and waved at the door.

After a few seconds, the door opened and an old woman stepped inside.

"You called Pack Lea- What happened in here!?"

Woodrow motioned to the brown werewolf, which seemed to have shrunk slightly in size.

"Jack got drugged with something that made him transform. Had a bit of a scuffle. I need you to go get the doctor, and gather a couple of Alpha class to help me take care of him. The doctor goes to bed early, so you may have to wake him. Whatever Alphas are still awake is fine. Also," Woodrow spared a glance to Angelica. "Bring our vampire guest a bottle of the good Irish whiskey."

The old woman bowed and left, closing the door behind her.

"Thanks beforehand for the drink. Also, make sure your doctor puts this guy on a full antibiotic treatment." Angelica waved at Jack, who was quickly transforming back to normal now.

Woodrow nodded.

"Don't worry, I know. Besides, werewolf bites might not be as bad as vampire bites, but they are still pretty nasty in their own right."

Angelica chuckled, running her fingers through her hair to try and get it under control. After a moment she frowned.

"After I accept that drink, I have to leave."

Woodrow frowned, leaning up against the wall and crossing his arms over his bare chest.

"Is there something you need to do? Based on the pace you have been keeping, I don't suppose you have had much rest lately. Are you sure you shouldn't take a break?"

Angelica shook her head.

"I saw some of this kid's recent memories. I know who gave him the drug, and why. I need to go take care of it immediately. We can't let him get away and hand out more of this stuff."

Woodrow huffed, shaking his head.

"Well, I won't tell you what to do, but what about your husband? Won't he expect to find you hereabouts?"

Angelica shook herself, pushing aside her desire to wait for Alaric.

"I am sure Alaric will return here eventually. Could you please tell him what happened and that I am going to the Elder Hive?"

Woodrow let out a deep sigh.

"Very well, I will pass the message along. As long as you stick around long enough for that drink."

Angelica smiled, resisting the urge to spit again.

"Well, I need to wash this taste out of my mouth somehow."

9

Chapter Nine

Alaric stood quietly in the forest clearing, waiting patiently for an escort to arrive. He shaded his eyes, looking up at the strange blueish-green sky. Some white clouds were drifting by, but their shapes twisted and changed unnaturally as they passed.

The forest was silent, though a gentle breeze seemed to carry the sounds of voices through the trees. After a short while, a small female voice called out.

"Are you lost, mister? Need some help?"

Alaric turned to find a fairy with a small, human-like figure, floating in the air at face level a few feet away. The figure had relatively long blonde hair and wore clothing made out of tree leaves tied together with blades of grass. Two pairs of wings, much like a dragonfly's, sprouted from their back, buzzing back and forth to keep them aloft.

They watched Alaric with metallic blue eyes that had no pupil or iris.

Alaric bowed slightly.

"No, I came to the Wilds of my own will. Though, I do appreciate your concern. I have something of great import I must discuss with your King and Queen. Might I graciously ask that you conduct me to them with all haste?"

The fairy crossed their arms over their chest and scratched their chin with one hand.

"I think their Majesties are quite busy today. I'm not sure they will have time to see you for at least a few decades."

Alaric bowed a little deeper.

"Please, if they could make time for me now, it is of great importance. It concerns a Pact they made with a large number of people in the human world. It could be broken, and a great many innocents could come to harm. I am certain that the King and Queen would be greatly put out to learn the loss of such a contract was likely."

The fairy frowned.

"Most would happily jump at the chance to break their contract. Why would you come here to try and save it?"

Alaric grinned, making sure to bare his fangs.

"I am one of those affected by the Pact and, I assure you, far worse things await us both if we allow the Pact to break."

The fairy flinched back.

"A vampire? Oh, well, that does complicate things. Alright, I will take you to the Royal Court, but I won't promise your intrusion will be welcomed. It's not my fault if you die."

Alaric bowed a little deeper once again and then stood upright.

"Any consequence is mine to bear. No one else is responsible."

The fairy nodded and turned around, waving their arm.

"Alright, follow me then. Try to keep up, you never know if someone here might get hungry."

Alaric nodded politely and followed close behind as the fairy flew away.

The fairy flew into the vegetation that surrounded the clearing and it seemed to part to reveal a small game trail. They followed it into the dense forest and Alaric could feel eyes all around him, watching silently as they passed.

They traveled what Alaric would have estimated to be several miles before the fairy paused and turned around, holding a tiny finger against their lips. Alaric nodded and they slowly entered a very large meadow.

The meadow itself was filled with short grasses and innumerable unique flowers in every shade of every color imaginable. At the opposite end of the meadow stood an oak tree with a trunk bigger than most sports stadiums, and with branches that easily reached ten times the height of the surrounding forest.

They carefully traveled the length of the meadow and, as they approached the great oak, Alaric saw two large figures lounging at the base of the tree.

On the right side of the tree, nestled among some roots that had grown in the shape of a large chair, sat a fifteen-foot-tall satyr. He had the upper body of a muscular man, with hair and a long beard the same color as the bark he sat on, and the lower half of a goat covered in fur that was a slightly darker brown.

On the left side of the tree, lounging on a couch of flowers, was a woman with fair skin and platinum blonde hair. She wore a long, flowing dress of a very light green color that seemed to have flowers of various colors growing from it. Though she was lying down, it was apparent that she was likely even taller than the satyr.

The woman was slowly petting an enormous deer, larger than a bus, with antlers that could have easily fit a small car between them. She was the first to notice Alaric and the fairy approaching, and the barest moment of annoyance appeared on her face before she smiled politely.

The satyr took notice and sat up. Alaric noticed a large wooden mug in his hand.

"What do we have here? I thought we were going to be having a wine tasting today. We weren't supposed to be entertaining any guests."

The fairy froze in the air, and Alaric dropped to one knee.

"Apologies, Great King, but this vampire said there was something important to discuss about their contract."

The woman tipped her head to one side, inspecting Alaric with her sharp hazel eyes. She waved for the small fairy to leave.

"It's been a little while since we have seen the vampires here, are you not content with the terms of the contract?"

Alaric shook his head, keeping it bowed.

"No, My Queen, we vampires still find the terms of the Pact we made to be most agreeable. I came to apologize on behalf of all because one of our kind is trying to find a way to sever the Pact. It is not something we wish for, Your Majesties, so I wish to beg your forgiveness and leniency to those who are innocent if that individual attempts any such thing."

"You seek to speak for all vampires, and yet ask that all vampires not be held accountable for the actions of another?" The satyr scowled down at Alaric.

Alaric nodded.

"We seek to stop the one who has made this wish, but I did not want his actions to be taken as the desire of our kind. Especially since our Elder Council went to such great lengths and personal risk once before to negotiate a change to that Pact already."

The woman tipped her head the other way.

"Have we yet met, young vampire?"

Alaric dared to raise his head a little and smiled.

"I have been in your presence once before, My Queen. Over five hundred years ago now, I escorted Elder Amalia and Elder Olbrecht to discuss a minor change to our Pact. Though Elder Olbrecht has since passed from his Curse."

The satyr leaned further forward, squinting at Alaric.

"Is that so?"

Alaric nodded, bowing his head again.

"It is, My King."

The woman carefully sat up on the couch.

"My King and My Queen sounds so impersonal. I would rather you refer to me as…" The woman paused to think for a moment. "Titania. I am fond of that name."

The satyr turned his head to look at the woman.

"From that bard's play?" He turned back to Alaric. "Then you should refer to me as Oberon."

Alaric bowed his head a bit lower.

"Lord Oberon, Lady Titania. I am Alaric."

Titania slid forward on her couch and placed her bare feet on the soft grass in front of her. She stood but, as she raised herself up, her size diminished until she had achieved the size of a normal human. She glided gracefully across the meadow and knelt down beside Alaric.

She raised her hand to his face and lifted his head to meet her gaze.

"What would you be willing to give me, in return for leniency for your people?"

Alaric met her gaze unflinchingly.

"What would you consider acceptable, Lady Titania?"

Titania smiled at him.

"Would you stay here, with me?"

Alaric smiled in return, but gently shook his head.

"I am sorry, Lady Titania. That is the one thing I cannot grant you."

Titania frowned, but then noticed something and slid her hand down to his neck. She pushed aside his coat collar and found the two white scars on the side of his neck.

"You have someone special to you?"

Alaric nodded.

"I do. I cannot, and will not, abandon her."

"Even if it means abandoning your people and earning our ire?" Oberon asked, leaning down and resting his elbow on one knee.

Alaric looked up at the satyr, his eyes flashing a sharp blue with a faint golden light shining deep behind his pupils.

"Even if I must leave here empty-handed. Even if I must hope that my skill alone can stop the one who plots against you before he succeeds. Even if it means me and my kind must face repercussions. Even if I must abandon all else, I will never allow her to be left alone."

Titania smiled again.

"What a wonderful thing love is. It makes me happy to hear you are so committed to her." Titania turned to look at Oberon with a slight pout. "Is there not something we can, perhaps, do? He seems sincere, and I like the conviction in his eyes."

Oberon sighed, setting aside his mug.

"If you are going to give me that look." He jumped from his seat and shrank to the size of a human before he hit the ground. He trotted over and squatted down in front of Alaric.

"Tell me, what is going on in your world?"

Alaric nodded politely.

"Some time ago some of our cousins, the werewolves, transformed outside of a full moon or Wild Hunt. When we inspected them we found they had been experimented on to change them outside their normal time. We discovered what was used on them came from one of our own, a somewhat younger member of our Elder Council. When I investigated him personally, not only did he try to poison me and my Bloodbonded, but I believe he was likely trying to use the werewolves as an experiment to figure out how to suppress our Cursed Blood. Then one of his personal servants, who he mistreated, told me he had discussed breaking our Pact with you. He likely believes that, if he can control the Cursed Blood, he can 'free' us from the Pact of The Fey. Namely, that which we have with you, Lord Oberon, and you, Lady Titania."

Titania and Oberon exchanged glances.

"So you believe he will do this soon?"

Alaric shook his head.

"Unfortunately, I cannot say exactly. He could be prepared to try already, or he may still be trying to complete his formulas. However I cannot say that, regardless of his preparedness, he will not attempt such a thing when I confront him. I wished to inform you of this to try and protect those who do not deserve punishment if that should come to pass."

Titania placed a hand on Oberon's knee.

"Is there not some way we can reconcile this? It seems that only the one wishes to break free. The others happily keep their promises."

Oberon scratched at his chin.

"Our contract is for all of vampire kind. Should any try to break it, it will break it for all. I am certain you understand the severity of such a thing."

Alaric nodded.

"I am old enough to remember the last of those who were not protected under the Pact. Those like Elder Olbrecht. Their deaths notwithstanding, our Curse will leave permanent scars on our world if it is not contained. And those scars will get reflected into yours."

Oberon nodded, glancing over his shoulder at a pale strip of dead bark high up on the trunk of the great oak.

"It is good to see that you understand." He paused for a few moments, then turned back to Alaric. "I can think of but one way to allow what you seek."

Alaric bowed his head again and waited.

"When you have exposed this vampire, and stopped him, we will take him and he will be brought to be punished here. However, we must have something from you as well. Something less substantial, but something that will bind our agreement."

Titania clasped her hands together excitedly.

"Oh, I know. You and your special one can join us for the next Midsummer Feast. I would be delighted to meet the one you would choose over everyone else."

Oberon stroked his beard, a grin forming under it.

"That would be acceptable. What say you, vampire Alaric?"

Alaric looked up, expressing his own grin.

"So long as we are not changed, and are both permitted to leave at feast's end, I will agree."

Oberon's grin grew wider, and he held out his hand.

"Then we have an agreement."

Alaric accepted the handshake.

"Excellent. Now, as I do not see a Feystone or a Key of any kind on your person, I am most curious how you intend to return to your world."

Alaric felt a corner of his mouth trying to widen his grin further.

"I will return the same way I came, through the use of high sorcery."

Oberon shook himself, and Titania placed a hand carefully over her mouth in surprise.

"I have never heard of a vampire capable of any sorcery, let alone the kind necessary to traverse realms."

Alaric nodded.

"Indeed. As far as is known, I am the only vampire who has ever been able to use sorcery. Most likely because our Cursed Blood and Fey Pact disrupt our human blood too much to allow us a strong connection to our world. However, my human blood carries a potential that even I must, unfortunately, describe as exceptional. It is possible that so much magic flowing through me pushes aside even my Curse."

Titania stood, clasping her hands at her waist.

"Have you interacted at all with the Human World's Academy for Sorcerers?" She asked, Oberon standing as well while she spoke.

Alaric also stood, finally allowing himself to genuinely smile.

"I have. One of the few outside of vampire kind that I would call a friend is currently a Headmaster for several branches of The Academy."

"Then have you been through their ceremonies? Have you drawn their cards? I would be most curious about what you drew." Oberon crossed his arms over his chest as he spoke.

Alaric nodded.

"I did. If it will aid in banishing any doubts you have about me, I am willing to show you. Though among my own kind, and other humans, I would wish to keep my own strength secret."

Oberon nodded.

"Understandable. Humans, of any kind, react poorly to power. Either seeking to worship it, or destroy it."

Alaric nodded once again then waved his hand, palm down, in front of his body. Three, ornately decorated, cards appeared face down in his hand. He turned his hand over and held them out to be inspected.

Titania gasped, placing one hand over her mouth once again, and Oberon's leg fur visibly bristled.

"Three Aces!? Even among human sorcerers, I believe that is unheard of."

Alaric nodded yet again, waving his hand and causing the cards to vanish once more.

"In the current human world, I am one of only seven, the world over, who has drawn such. You can see now why I believe my human blood is strong enough to overcome even the Cursed Blood."

Oberon nodded, starting to grin again.

"Indeed. Perhaps you are correct. At any rate, please feel free to use this meadow to return to your realm. I rarely get to witness true human sorcery."

Alaric bowed.

"Then I will take my leave. Lord Oberon, Lady Titania. You have my gratitude for hearing me out, and allowing me to come to an agreement."

Oberon nodded and Titania waved goodbye.

Alaric turned and walked a short way away from them to give him plenty of space.

As he had in the basement of Elder Jayin's estate, Alaric held his arms out with his palms turned upwards.

He began speaking a spell and a golden aura surrounded him like a shallow golden flame. The air in the meadow began to move, lifting blades of grass and flower petals in a kaleidoscope of color that swirled around him like a whirlwind.

Alaric's eyes began glowing gold, and he spoke in a voice that resonated across the meadow.

"The material world, I seek. On solid earth, let my feet land firm."

Glowing, golden vines reached up from the ground, forming an archway in the air before him. The image that was the meadow behind the archway peeled away, revealing a blank nothingness. After a few moments, the nothingness was filled with light, which quickly faded away to reveal the basement that Alaric had traveled from originally.

Alaric lowered his arms, his golden aura fading away. He stepped through the archway and, as it began to disappear, he turned and bowed once more to Oberon and Titania.

The archway disappeared completely, leaving the Fey King and Queen standing alone.

"Fascinating. I think that, perhaps, bending the rules for him was a perfect choice." Titania turned as she spoke, returning to pet the nose of her deer.

Oberon nodded, a skip and a hop returning him to full size and landing him back in his seat.

"I think he will be a most interesting individual to interact with. We will have to watch him closely, to see how things play out. I think we can have all sorts of fun with him."

Titania nuzzled her face against the deer, choosing to stay human-sized for the time being.

"Someone as intelligent as him should, indeed, be fun. And I also want to meet the one he holds special above all."

Oberon laughed, finding his wooden mug and taking a long drink from it.

"Don't get jealous, my love. She has already taken him from you after all."

Titania pouted.

"I can't help it, but I still want to meet her."

10

Chapter Ten

Angelica stood outside the main council chamber doors, the guards standing on either side of the door ignoring her completely.

She could hear someone speaking to the council inside, their voice echoing throughout the chamber. The echoes and door made it hard to hear, but from what she could understand she decided they must be discussing the building of a new Hive somewhere.

Angelica stood quietly, trying not to shuffle around anxiously. She went over what she would say when she accused Elder Jayin, repeating the words in her head so she wouldn't forget them in the moment. She started wondering if she should have waited for Alaric to make a more convincing argument.

A new subject was now being discussed beyond the door, but Angelica couldn't pick out enough information to figure out what it was. The air in the Elder Hive was cool and dry, but she was starting to feel hot. She found herself tugging at the collar of the dress coat that identified her as a Suite Lord, hoping it would cool her down.

Another hour passed, two more subjects being discussed that Angelica didn't care enough about to listen to. She waited, trying to be patient, until one of the guards opened the door and motioned her inside.

The Council chamber was a large circular room, about a hundred feet across, with a slightly raised platform in the center for people who would address the Council. The room was surrounded by an eight-foot-high elevated dais with two rows of seats, with one section having only three raised single seats for the Council leaders. A dozen or so other Elders were dotted around the other seats in the room.

Angelica entered the chamber, walking forward and stepping up onto the platform in the center of the room. This was only the second time she had ever set foot in the council chamber, but nothing seemed to have changed in the two hundred years since she had last been here.

She turned to face the three Council leaders and found Elder Amalia, Elder Mihail, and Elder Jayin looking back at her.

Elder Amalia sat in the center seat, her seat on a platform raised slightly higher than the others so that her head was level with the other two. Her hair was pulled up in a tight bun on top of her head and a short length of loose hair fanned out from the back of the bun.

Elder Mihail, aside from his bright red council robes, looked almost exactly the same as he had back when Angelica had met him in Germany, several days before.

Elder Jayin was an average-looking man who appeared to be middle-aged. He had tan skin and gray eyes and wore a council robe that was a slightly darker shade than the other two Elders.

Angelica made sure she was standing at the center of the raised platform and bowed to the council leaders.

"Suite Lord Angelica of the Great Plains Hive, we have been informed that you had a matter of great importance that needed to be brought before the council immediately."

Elder Amalia's voice echoed across the council chamber, far more serious than it had been at her estate.

"What has brought you here that required you to ask to be brought before us with such haste?"

Elder Mihail's voice did not echo as much as Amalia's, but it seemed to pierce through those who heard it.

Angelica stood, back straight, trying to emulate what she thought Alaric would do.

"I beg the Elder Council's forgiveness for my hasty arrival, but information has come to light that demands immediate action. A member of this council has betrayed its trust, and they must answer for their crimes."

Angelica did her best to keep her eyes on Elder Amalia but tried to use her peripheral vision to see if Elder Jayin reacted.

"That is a very serious accusation to bring here." Elder Jayin stated. "There are dire consequences for false accusations against an Elder. Are you certain that what information you have is without flaw?"

Angelica raised her chin, trying to stand taller, and gave a short nod.

"There are witnesses and I have seen memories of one who interacted with this individual."

"Memories? Have you bitten someone, Suite Lord?" Elder Amalia asked.

Angelica nodded.

"I was given no choice. The memories flowing through me were merely an accidental side effect of the action I was forced to take. If there is still too great of concern over the matter, the one I bit was a Curse-Blood."

"These details we will inquire of later." Elder Mihail responded. "Who is it you are making this accusation against?"

Angelica carefully raised her arm, hand open and palm faced up, indicating Elder Jayin.

"I am here to accuse Elder Jayin of conspiracy against the council."

Elder Jayin scowled, but Elder Amalia motioned towards the open floor.

"Elder Jayin, please join Suite Lord Angelica on the platform so that we may get to the heart of this matter."

Elder Jayin stood, sweeping the sleeves of his robe behind him and quickly moving down the stairs of the dais and out onto the platform.

"What conspiracy do you believe I have committed against this Council of Elders?" Elder Jayin asked, keeping his hands clasped behind his back.

Angelica spared a moment to look the man up and down, then looked up at Elder Amalia and Elder Mihail again.

"I have come here to accuse Elder Jayin of unauthorized possession of pure Quintessence crystals, experimentation on our fellow Curse-Bloods, attempted poisoning of myself and Lord Alaric, unnecessary cruelty, and plotting to have the Pack Leader of the London Enclave assassinated."

"A substantial list of accusations." Elder Amalia stated, her fierce eyes boring a hole through Angelica. "I hope you have evidence to substantiate these claims."

Angelica nodded.

"I do. As the Council may be aware, a short time ago the Great Plains Hive lost its Overlord. This was due to the fact that he took Quintessence, without permission or authorization, and shipped it directly to Elder Jayin's estate."

"This is the first I am hearing of such a shipment." Elder Jayin claimed. "Are you certain that he told you the truth?"

Angelica glanced at Elder Jayin, trying to swallow her dislike for the man.

"He only revealed the truth under the command of Hivelord Andros. I do not believe it is possible for a Lord to lie to an Archlord that has commanded them."

Elder Jayin simply nodded.

"Very well, continue with your 'evidence' then."

Angelica frowned, looking back up at Elder Amalia.

"During our tour of Europe, my Blood-bonded Alaric and I stopped to pay our respects to Elder Jayin. Unfortunately, that was shortly after the Elder was called to council. At the instruction of Elder Jayin, his servants invited us in for the evening meal. When the drinks were served to us, we found that they were poisoned. The servant who brought the drinks, when it was caught, admitted that Elder Jayin had instructed them to poison us. When asked why, they showed us to a hidden basement study, where we found most of the Quintessence that had gone missing from the Great Plains Hive."

Elder Jayin paced a few steps to one side.

"How could you know these servants acted on my orders? How were you somehow able to tell the drinks were poisoned? If they, indeed, were. How can you be certain that this 'hidden study' was mine, and not created by the maid who took you there to try and set me up to be deposed from my seat on the Council?"

Angelica's eyes flicked over and locked with Elder Jayin's.

"I never once mentioned it was a maid who showed us the study."

Elder Jayin raised his hand and pointed directly at Angelica, his eyes flashing red.

"That's enough."

His voice struck Angelica with an almost physical force. She felt her vision fading, and control of her body was wrested from her.

"I have heard enough of these baseless accusations." Elder Jayin slowly walked forward as he spoke. "Everything you call evidence is merely hearsay and bias. Clearly meant as an attempt to make me look bad in front of this council. I don't know if you or Lord Alaric are trying to take my place on the council, but I will not allow such disrespect to the honor I have spent centuries earning."

As he approached Angelica, Elder Jayin opened his hand like a claw and reached for her heart.

In a fraction of a moment, faster than any eye could see, a hand clamped down on Elder Jayin's outstretched wrist.

"You will not lay a hand on my Blood-bonded."

Alaric stood beside Elder Jayin, his silver hair floating and glowing with an otherworldly light, a dense golden aura surrounding him like a burning flame. A split second after he spoke, four guards had surrounded him, holding their arms out like blades towards him.

Elder Jayin growled, his eyes glowing a bright blood red.

"Release me." The four guards faltered as the Elder's command struck them.

Alaric merely smirked bitterly.

"Your command cannot reach me, Elder."

Elder Jayin was taken aback, his eyes returning back to normal.

"That isn't possible. There isn't a Lord alive who can resist my command."

"That's because Lord Alaric is an old Archlord-class vampire. Nearly as old as yourself, in fact, Jayin." Elder Amalia spoke, now standing. "Do not make the mistake of thinking you can bully him with a simple command as easily as you do others. Release him, Alaric. Lord Angelica will remain with me until you have finished presenting your arguments."

Elder Jayin realized that, somehow, Elder Amalia had taken Angelica and placed her in the center council seat without his notice. She now stood beside the seat, with one hand resting protectively on Angelica's shoulder.

Alaric slowly released Elder Jayin's wrist, his hair returning to normal and his aura fading away.

"Guards, your services are not needed at this time." Elder Mihail stated, also standing from his seat.

The guards all bowed to Elder Mihail and then quickly disappeared.

"Now, please continue with your accusations and evidence." Elder Mihail motioned to Alaric. "I am sorry to say that so far, the evidence is circumstantial. Elder Jayin is correct. We will need better evidence than that to be able to determine if action should be taken. At most, a minor investigation is all that is warranted at this time."

Alaric bowed.

"Then allow me to begin where my Blood-bonded left off. The servants themselves told us, when we arrived, that Elder Jayin had invited us for the evening meal. I knew the drinks were poisoned, firstly because of how the maid who served us acted when she brought them. Secondly, upon inspection, I could smell both nightshade and colloidal silver in the drinks. It was particularly pronounced in the hot tea. Upon questioning, the maid was terrified of her master and had to be gently coaxed to answer. She led us to the study only after being assured she would be taken away from Elder Jayin. That, in and of itself, is not evidence enough of course. Though I again bring up Angelica's comment. Not once did she ever state that it was a maid that did these things, or even a female for that matter. How is it that Elder Jayin knew this?"

Elder Jayin scoffed.

"That is hardly more convincing than the girl."

Alaric spared Elder Jayin an unreadable look then looked back to the other two Elders.

"The maid who spoke with us has been conducted safely to Elder Mihail's estate. Should you wish to question her yourself, she is waiting there. She also carries with her a package with the missing Quintessence that can only be opened by Elder Mihail himself. I am certain the only fingerprints you will find on the container within will be mine and Elder Jayin's."

Alaric paused a moment before taking a breath and continuing.

"On that same subject, Overlord Burchard should have arrived here by now. You may also wake him and interview him yourselves to discover his role in this. This leads us to our second accusation, experimentation on Curse-Bloods. The night after this past full moon, two Waif class werewolves transformed and attacked someone. They were contained before they caused any deaths, but died in the altercation."

"What does that have to do with me?" Elder Jayin spat.

Alaric didn't even bother to look at the Elder and continued.

"When they were tested, both Waifs were found to have a host of drugs and Quintessence in their blood. I had the test results verified by Master Faust here at the Elder Hive and, by now, I am sure Elder Mihail has a copy of that report. The mixture of drugs seemed to have been created to attack Cursed Blood and cause werewolves to frenzy and transform. The only Quintessence that has left the Great Plains Hive, that was not confirmed to have arrived at the Elder Hive by Master Faust, was that which was taken by Overlord Burchard and sent to Elder Jayin."

"What do I possibly stand to gain from this?" Elder Jayin turned to the other Elder's and waved his hand at Alaric.

"I grow tired of your constant interruptions." Alaric stated, a dangerous glint in his eyes, in a tone that caused even Jayin to take a moment of pause.

Elder Amalia nodded.

"Please be silent, Jayin. You may give your defense when Alaric is done with his accusations."

Alaric bowed his head to Elder Amalia.

"Firstly, as a counter to the argument that the maid may have done this out of spite, she would not have had the time, nor the expertise, to craft such a drug. Secondly, a similar drug was used yesterday evening by an Alpha-class werewolf at the London Enclave to transform. His stated purpose was to kill Pack Leader Woodrow, though Angelica was also present at that time and he attacked her as well.

He was saved only because Angelica bit him and was able to draw the drug from his blood while Pack Leader Woodrow held him down. Pack Leader Woodrow told me what transpired, and that Angelica had left shortly after biting him, claiming she had seen who had given that young werewolf the drug. As she hurried here without even waiting for me, and accused Elder Jayin without hesitation, I would presume he was the one she saw. I brought a sample of the drug from London with me, and have already given it to Master Faust. I would guess that it will be discovered to be almost identical to what was found in the two Waifs in the United States."

Elder Amalia looked down at Angelica.

"Is that true, Lord Angelica?"

Angelica nodded carefully.

"Elder Jayin gave the young man the drug, with the express instructions to use it to ambush and kill Pack Leader Woodrow."

Amalia nodded and looked back down at the floor below.

"What have you to say in your defense, Jayin?"

Elder Jayin growled angrily.

"Again I ask, What would I possibly have to gain from any of this? Why would I go to such lengths to do any of this? Creating a drug to make werewolves change. Stealing Quintessence that I can already receive here, at the Elder Hive. There is no sense in any of these actions. If anything, I would believe these two lords are simply trying to take my place. Nothing else makes sense."

"I have already been offered a seat in the Elder Council." Alaric stated flatly. "Several times in fact. Each time I have refused the position. I need not remove you from your seat to receive my own if I so wish."

Elder Jayin spun around to point at Alaric.

"I will not hear more of your lies."

"It is no lie, Jayin." Elder Amalia stated. "I have offered Alaric a seat on the council multiple times during the last few centuries. His place is already assured if he ever chooses to accept it."

There was muttering among the other Elders and Elder Jayin turned again, a look of unpleasant surprise on his face.

Elder Amalia frowned.

"That said, it is difficult to imagine Elder Jayin doing any of this without reason. We can order an investigation, as a vampire was witnessed biting this werewolf and has claimed to see Elder Jayin in his memories. But that does not prove malicious intent. In order to prove he has done anything deliberately wrong, we must have a reason for these actions to have been taken in direct opposition to the will of the Elder Council."

Alaric sighed, a deeply unhappy expression on his face.

"His reason is far worse than you can imagine, Elders. It is also the reason I arrived later than Lord Angelica. The same maid that showed us the study brought it to my attention, insisting others in the estate also knew. Upon questioning several, I determined they were under the same impression as she. His goal is to break our Pact with the King and Queen of the Fey."

A ripple of gasps traveled through the handful of other Elders present, and both Amalia and Mihail scowled.

"To even suggest such a thing could, itself, be considered rebellion against the Pact." Mihail stated. "Are you most certain of this claim?"

Alaric nodded firmly.

"I am. You may investigate these claims yourself, as I have spoken of each of my sources for these claims. It was also discussed between Elder Jayin and an unknown third party. I have yet to discover this third party, but everyone at the estate was certain that a visitor had come multiple times to speak with Elder Jayin. Elder Jayin held all of them each time, and blinded them, but not all of them were deafened. They heard what was spoken of and now each of his servants fears him and any strangers that visit. Never certain who might be the one their master had spoken with."

"Lies, all of it!" Elder Jayin yelled, waving angrily at Alaric. "I insist that these accusers be locked up and punished for this incredibly slanderous tall tail."

Angelica clenched her fists in her lap, trying not to scream in anger. After a moment of struggle, she looked up at Amalia desperately.

"May I please say something?"

Elder Amalia looked down at Angelica, inspecting her eyes carefully. After a moment she nodded.

"I don't know what more we can do, but say your piece."

Angelica turned back, looking down at Alaric with tears of frustration in her eyes.

"Don't let him do this. Don't let him hurt anyone else. You gave me a wish in Paris. Fulfill my wish now. Stop holding back. Force him to tell the truth!" Angelica was almost screaming by the end and her voice caught in her throat.

Elder Jayin turned red in the face.

"Shut your mouth, you noisy peasant."

An enormous pressure washed over the room in a wave of golden light and each of the Elders slumped over in their seats. Even Amalia and Mihail had to brace themselves to remain upright under the immense pressure.

"You will not speak to my Blood-bonded in such a manner again."

Alaric's voice rolled over the room, deep and resonant, demanding obedience. His bright golden aura had returned, waving around him in an angrily burning flame, and his eyes now glowed a fiery red. The air in the room began to press against those present as if it had suddenly gained tremendous weight.

"Face me, Jayin."

Jayin flinched as Alaric's command pierced his ears and mind. He haltingly turned and faced Alaric, his arms held tightly at his side.

"Did you do the things you have been accused of today?"

Jayin struggled, his face contorting in frustration.

"Yes." He growled through gritted teeth.

"Did you seek to break the Pact?"

Jayin bared his fangs, trying to move.

"Yes."

"With whom did you conspire?"

Jayin tried to turn his face away, but Alaric's eyes and fierce expression held him in place.

"A...Sorcerer."

Alaric frowned deeply.

"What does he receive in return?"

Jayin scowled, growling like a cornered animal.

"Access... to..." He tried to stop himself from speaking, yelling in frustration as the words escaped his lips. "The... Library!"

Alaric's frown turned into a dangerous scowl.

"Kneel."

The command struck Jayin with such force that he dropped to his knees as if his legs had been pulled from under him.

Alaric held his arm out to one side.

"Alaric, no! Don't harm him!" Elder Amalia called out over the council room.

"He will not die by my hand." Alaric stated emotionlessly, pointing at the far wall. "By our agreement, My King, this soul is yours. Claim it, if you so wish to have it."

Alaric's voice rang hollow, as if muffled or spoken underwater. After several seconds, a rumble began to shake the council chambers.

From across the room, where Alaric was pointing, a tear seemed to form in the air. The tear grew, becoming longer and wider with each passing moment. After several seconds it had grown as tall as a house, and wide enough for several people to pass through side by side.

Another moment passed by, then a fifteen-foot-tall figure stepped through into the council room.

Elder Amalia gasped in surprise and quickly bowed, Elder Mihail immediately following her example.

"My King, I was not aware you would grace us with your presence on this day."

The tall satyr stretched with a groan, then took a deep breath.

"Long has it been since I last stepped foot in this world. The air doesn't seem as clean as it used to be."

Elder Amalia nodded, not raising her head.

"Indeed. Humankind has grown large since your last visit here. We pollute the air far more than we used to. To what do we owe the honor of your visit, My King?"

The satyr looked around before spotting Alaric, and trotting over to him.

"Is this the one causing the troubles you spoke of?"

Alaric nodded, his eyes still glowing, maintaining complete control over Jayin.

"He is the one trying to break the Pact, Lord Oberon. We have heard it spoken from his own mouth."

Oberon nodded, reaching down and lifting Jayin off the floor in one hand.

Alaric's eyes returned to normal, but his aura remained.

Jayin struggled after he was released for a moment before he realized where he was. He froze and stared up into Oberon's face, his mouth moving wordlessly in terror.

Muttering and mumbling rippled around the room, followed by gasps and bowing as the other Elders came to.

Angelica groaned and shook herself, trying to clear her head.

Oberon glanced up and grinned, his eyes sparkling mischievously.

"Is she the one, vampire Alaric?"

Alaric nodded, careful to keep his hand pointed directly at the tear that was still open along the far wall.

"She is my Blood-bonded, Lord Oberon. Please be gentle with her. It will take a moment for all of her senses to return."

Oberon trotted excitedly over to the dais and held his large, unoccupied, hand out in front of Angelica.

"Good morning to you, young vampire. You may call me Oberon. By what name might I know you?"

Angelica looked up at the large hand, a few moments of confusion suddenly giving way to shocking clarity.

"I-I am Angelica. It is a true honor to make your acquaintance, Lord Oberon." She carefully placed a hand on one of Oberon's fingers, not certain what was expected of her.

Oberon grinned happily and carefully shook Angelica's hand.

"And I am pleased to make yours, vampire Angelica. My wife will be so jealous when she hears of this."

Oberon trotted back towards the tear, chuckling giddily to himself.

"Vampire Alaric, our agreement is acceptably fulfilled. No harm will come to your people so long as they continue to honor their contract. I also very much enjoyed the vigor with which you jumped to your lady's defense. For that entertainment, please consider asking a boon of me when next we meet. I look forward to seeing you and your special one, and hearing what boon you have come up with, at midsummer."

Oberon waved with the hand that held Jayin, who was tossed around like a rag doll, then skipped through the open tear.

Alaric muttered a few words and closed his fist, the tear following his command and closing up, the wall returning to normal as if nothing had been there at all.

Elder Amalia sighed in relief and stood up straight. She carefully placed a hand on Angelica's back.

"You can go to him now."

Angelica shook herself out of her state of shock and nodded, standing.

"Thank you, Elder."

Angelica rushed down to the platform, jumping up and practically throwing herself into Alaric's arms. She buried her face against Alaric's chest and wrapped her arms around him as tightly as she could manage.

"Why did the King of The Fey just shake my hand?"

"I would also like to have an answer to that question, Alaric."

Elder Amalia gracefully descended from the dais and approached the platform.

Alaric nodded tiredly.

"It will be a long story. Perhaps we should go somewhere we can sit down and speak at length."

Elder Amalia nodded, turning around and addressing the rest of the Council.

"We will conclude this meeting until we can learn more of what has happened today. Please return to your rooms, but stay at the Elder Hive until such a time that we can guarantee another council session will not be needed."

The other Elders all bowed and stood, filtering their way out of the room.

Elder Mihail approached Elder Amalia.

"We may speak in my chambers. They are nearest and I have far less decoration than you, Lady Amalia."

Elder Amalia nodded.

"Yes, very well. I am expecting to get a full explanation, Alaric."

Alaric nodded, gently pushing Angelica away from him.

"I will do my best to make everything clear."

11

Chapter Eleven

Angelica stood behind Alaric, leaning over the back of the loveseat to gently massage his neck and shoulders.

Amalia sat quietly in an armchair across from them with a very serious face, making no effort to try and use her childish facade.

Mihail stood nearby, facing a painting of a mountainous landscape covered in swirling mist.

"The most pressing question must be, why did the King of The Fey deign to interfere directly?" Mihail spoke but never turned away from the painting.

Angelica felt Alaric shift slightly beneath her hands.

"When I heard that it was likely that Elder Jayin was trying to break the Pact, I immediately went before the King and Queen of the Fey to beg for leniency. I did not want Elder Jayin to preemptively try to break the Pact and leave numerous innocents to pay the price of his betrayal. I was able to get Lord Oberon to agree on the condition that Elder Jayin be given to him, to face his punishment alone, once he was caught."

Angelica felt Alaric's neck growing tight and carefully rubbed the back of his neck with her thumbs.

"And you did not think this important enough to bring before us before accusing Jayin?" Amalia asked, clearly in an unpleasant mood.

"That was my mistake." Angelica answered, shaking her head. "When I saw the memories of the werewolf who attacked Pack Leader

Woodrow, I rushed here immediately. I was rash and did not stop to consider the consequences. I hadn't consulted with Alaric beforehand, and I did not know what he had gone to do. The fault for that is mine to bear, not Alaric's."

Mihail finally turned around with a sigh.

"I see. What, exactly, is it that you saw that caused you to run ahead without Lord Alaric?"

Angelica bowed, walking around the loveseat and sitting next to Alaric before answering.

"I saw the young werewolf standing before Elder Jayin. The Elder was questioning whether or not he was capable of taking a life. When the young werewolf insisted that he could, Elder Jayin pulled out a vial of a drug that would allow him to transform from his robes. He claimed that we should lock up Pure-Bloods during the full moon instead of the werewolves and that they needed to kill Pack Leader Woodrow to do that. When the young werewolf left, he had been made to feel like it was his destiny to achieve this end. I had already seen the fear in those who worked at Elder Jayin's estate, and this act was too much for me. I did not stop to consider the best course, I simply acted. Foolish as it may have been."

Mihail looked over to Amalia.

Amalia frowned.

"I see."

They sat in an uncomfortable silence for several minutes, Amalia clearly deliberating over a large amount of information.

Amalia sighed quietly and shook her head.

"As messy as this was, and as unpleasant as the methods were, Elder Jayin did admit to everything he was accused of. This still warrants an investigation, however, as there are loose ends that must be tied before we can call the matter closed."

Alaric nodded.

"I am most concerned about this sorcerer Elder Jayin referred to. The fact that the existence of The Library is known outside of the

Curse-Bloods at all is already cause for concern. There is also the fact that some amount of Quintessence is still missing. Enough to make five doses of the drug that can transform werewolves outside of their normal cycles. And with a sorcerer involved, some of that may have been taken away for something else entirely. Even a moderately proficient sorcerer could elevate their power immensely for a short time with even a small amount of what is still missing. Though, we are very fortunate that we discovered this plot when we did before it became a significantly greater issue."

Mihail frowned, his arms held behind his back.

"As a sorcerer yourself, what do you think our best course of action would be?"

Alaric leaned forward, resting his elbows on his knees and lacing his fingers together.

"We have to assume that this sorcerer will do his best to remain hidden until he chooses to act. Once word of Elder Jayin's disappearance gets out, he will likely either run or attempt to gain access to The Library on his own. In either case, I think it likely that The Library will be too great a temptation to resist forever. We should do our best to ensure it is sealed and protected against any attempt to enter that may wake the Origin Cursebearer."

Amalia tilted her head to one side.

"Is the seal we have, and the constant guard, not good enough?"

Alaric shook his head carefully.

"It was crafted by old Curse-Blood alchemists, not true sorcerers. To an average sorcerer perhaps it would be strong enough. However a more powerful sorcerer, or one trained for cursebreaking, could bypass the seal. And if the sorcerer we are looking for has Quintessence, his power will be anything but average. Until now, we have not had a need for new seals. Secrecy has been our greatest protection. However, thanks to Elder Jayin, that will no longer be sufficient."

Mihail slowly made his way to a chair next to Amalia and sat down.

"Would you be able to craft a more sufficient seal?"

Alaric shook his head again.

"I am not proficient with permanent magic, such as seals." He paused for a moment, looking down at his hands. The wheels in his head turning through the possibilities. "But, with the permission of the council, there are two individuals I know with unsurpassed knowledge of seals. They are connected to no country or group and are trustworthy and discreet. Both are capable of understanding why The Library must be protected at all costs."

Amalia frowned deeply.

"This is a matter we do not wish to make known to the Pure-Bloods."

Alaric nodded.

"I am well aware of the implications it could have, but an unknown number of Pure-Bloods have already been made aware of The Library's existence. And we will already have to make The Academy aware of the fact a sorcerer could be carrying an exceptionally potent catalyst. If the Quintessence is used in public, there will already be many sorcerers looking for the source of this catalyst. I have known the Headmasters in the United States for many years. They are trustworthy, and will be able to ensure that the problem is taken care of in a way that will not cause future problems for us."

Angelica leaned forward and placed one hand on Alaric's back.

"Could Orpheus also craft new seals for us?"

Alaric nodded.

"He could. There is not a more skilled sorcerer than Orpheus anywhere. However, there are two that are much closer to this part of the world who are more specialized in sealing magic."

Amalia shook her head.

"I still do not believe it is worth the risk to call for outside aid."

"I am afraid I must concur." Mihail stated. "We cannot risk unleashing another plague if The Library were to be opened and the Curse-bearer awakened. Sorcerers are known to be ambitious, and seekers of knowledge. As you yourself said, The Library is too great a temptation."

Alaric carefully lifted his hands and rubbed his face, Angelica giving him a worried look as he did. He sighed deeply and held one hand out, palm down.

"Not all of us sorcerers must seek knowledge to elevate our strength."

With a wave, three cards appeared in his hand.

"I am certain that, even among Curse-Bloods, the meaning of the cards used by The Academy are still understood."

Angelica's hand slid up to Alaric's shoulder.

"Are you sure? You have hidden them for so long."

After several moments of pause, Alaric nodded.

Amalia tilted her head again, this time a look of confusion on her face.

"Hidden? Why hide your cards? Do they not merely show your strengths and weaknesses?"

Alaric nodded again, turning over the cards.

"Some carry cards without weakness."

Amalia's small hands squeezed tightly on the arms of her chair, causing the wood beneath the upholstery to crack under the force, and Mihail very nearly leaped from his own chair.

Alaric spoke before either could comment.

"Those who carry cards like mine we refer to as Aces. Currently, there are only seven of us in the world. Myself, Master Orpheus of The Academy, Master Shepherd of Koyane Manor, Master Pendragon of England, Master Ahanna of India, Master Takanashi of Japan, and Master Varion who stays in no one place for very long."

Even Angelica found herself growing tense, realizing she was squeezing Alaric's shoulder tightly. She relaxed her hand but slid it further down his back again.

"Sorry for my surprise, My Love. I realized why you try not to speak so much of Master Orpheus and Master Shepherd now."

Alaric smiled sadly at Angelica, turning his hand over and causing his cards to disappear.

"Don't be sorry Angie, it's no real secret that they are unrivaled sorcerers. We are all just private by nature. The world is not kind to those with power. And even I must admit that those who draw three Aces are uniquely powerful."

"I knew you were special, but Aces..." Amalia muttered quietly before shaking herself. "No, it is of no consequence. You are still Alaric, all the same. We merely have a more perfect picture of you now."

Alaric bowed his head slightly.

"I am sorry, Elder Amalia, I have never wished to use my position in this way. But I felt it was important that I be understood when I say there are a very small few that I believe can be trusted with the knowledge of The Library, and can understand why it is necessary that it never be opened. Master Ahanna and Master Takanashi both specialize in sealing magic. Master Ahanna can be here in a day, and Master Takanashi in two. If they seal The Library for us, only one of the Seven Aces would ever be powerful enough to be able to get inside."

Mihail lowered himself back down into his chair.

"I must also apologize for my behavior. I should not have been taken by such surprise. Especially after witnessing your actions in the council chambers. There are few that I could claim to have a will equal to Lady Amalia's, but even I had trouble resisting your command."

Alaric bowed his head lower.

"That is high praise, Elder Mihail. However, I would never wish to enter a contest of wills with Elder Amalia."

Amalia sighed, choosing not to say anything about it. After a few moments, she made a decision.

"Very well. If you truly believe these two individuals will be willing to help us and can be trusted not to enter The Library, then you have my permission to call on them and invite them to the Elder Hive."

Mihail nodded.

"And you have my consent as well. Lady Amalia and I will address the council and explain the situation with the sorcerer. We will also seek approval for making contact with The Academy to warn them of a potential threat from this sorcerer."

Alaric sat up and nodded.

"Thank you, I will contact them as soon as I am able."

Amalia waved one hand, sighing again and laying back in her chair.

"We have few other viable options. Sadly, we have no other sorcerers among the Curse-Bloods. If we want to have more powerful defenses, eventually we would have to seek help from the outside. This situation has merely forced us to do what would likely have happened eventually anyway. Though, it would have taken far longer to decide if we had not had the push. So, I imagine we should be thanking you for being so insistent."

Alaric shook his head.

"No, The Library is a threat to more than just Curse-Bloods. I merely seek to protect those who cannot protect themselves. Well, I also can't help but want to protect Angie too, regardless of her ability to take care of herself."

Alaric looked over and grinned at Angelica.

Angelica pouted.

"One of these days I'll be the one protecting you. You'll see."

Amalia grinned, her expression taking on some of her childish quality.

"I will wish for your day to come, Lord Angelica."

Angelica seemed to remember there were other people present and her cheeks turned red.

Alaric stood, holding his hand out to Angelica. After a moment, she accepted it and allowed him to help her stand.

"We will beg your pardon and seek our room now, Elders." Alaric said, bowing.

Angelica bowed as well.

"Thank you for listening to me, even though I was not prepared." She said.

Mihail nodded.

"We have been wondering in what direction Elder Jayin has been trying to lead the council in recent times. Having that all brought to light has made things much simpler, in spite of the need to investigate all your claims. You have done us all a favor. Rest easy in that knowledge."

"With your leave." Alaric said.

Still holding Angelica's hand, Alaric led her to the door and opened it for her.

Once they were gone, and the door had closed behind them, Amalia slid off her chair and stretched with a small groan.

"Mihail, I think I will find my own room and take a long bath. We can call the other Elders back to council in the evening."

Mihail half bowed in his chair.

"I will ensure they are notified. Please enjoy your bath, Lady Amalia."

Amalia placed a finger on her lower lip as if she were carefully considering it.

"I think I shall." She said, before giggling and skipping towards the door.

She waved a few times and then opened the door and slipped through, leaving Mihail to sit peacefully in his, now quiet, room.

* * *

Alaric sat down on the end of the bed with an exaggerated groan. He placed his phone on the small set of drawers near the bed and then laid back on the bed covers.

"Were they willing to hear you out, My Love?" Angelica asked, peeking out of the bathroom where she was brushing her freshly washed and dried hair.

Alaric nodded, lifting his arm and placing it over his eyes.

"They were. I was not overly concerned that they would not, of course. Master Takanashi has always been a mellow and reasonable man, more so now that he has gotten older. I have not had more than a few interactions with Master Ahanna, but she is very intelligent and I was certain she would understand if I explained the situation."

"That is good to hear, the sooner the situation is taken care of the better."

Alaric felt Angelica climb onto the bed next to him. She gently took hold of his arm and pulled it away from his face, peering down at him.

"The room they are letting us use here is very nice, but I miss sleeping in our bed back at home."

Alaric smiled, looking Angelica up and down. After her shower, she had changed into a set of silk night clothes. They were loose fitting and, even though they were black, they had a subtle iridescent sheen.

"New clothes? You look beautiful."

Angelica's cheeks turned pink and she put her hands behind her head and posed on the bed.

"Do you like them? I thought the colors were pretty, so I bought them at a gift shop while I was waiting for a connecting train in Poland."

Alaric chuckled, reaching out and running his hand down Angelica's side.

"They aren't as pretty as you, but they do look nice. It feels like they would be comfortable too."

"They are." Angelica said, quickly laying down so she could trap Alaric's arm beneath her.

Alaric grinned, using the opportunity to pull her closer to him.

"When we leave, perhaps I will have to find a set for myself."

Angelica smiled contentedly, cuddling next to Alaric and placing one hand on his chest. They laid quietly for several minutes, enjoying the peaceful silence.

After a while, Angelica sighed.

"I am sorry I ran ahead without you. Thank you for coming to save me, My Love."

Alaric turned his head and kissed Angelica's forehead.

"You smell nice." He said, attempting to dodge the conversation.

Angelica pouted, stretching and kissing him before he could turn away.

"I mean it. I did something stupid and I made you worry. I am truly grateful you came to my rescue."

Alaric sighed, smiling sadly. He used his free hand to tilt her head up so he could rest his forehead against hers and look directly into her eyes.

"I know, Love. I won't chastise you for feeling hurt for those people. I felt the same way, but I had to try and save them from the future suffering Jayin was going to cause them. What you did was risky, but Elder Amalia wouldn't have let him harm you."

Angelica kissed Alaric again and then buried her face against his neck.

"I still should have waited. You worried so much for me that I can still feel your heart racing. If I had said something more angrily than I did he might have reacted more violently, and I already know how much you had to hold back not to harm him."

Alaric squeezed her, resting his head against hers.

"When it comes to you, I struggle to think of the consequences of acting. Nothing ever seems as important as protecting you. I am sorry for the trouble it causes you."

Angelica laughed softly.

"It's endearing. And you always restrain yourself. That restraint is one of the many reasons I love you." She paused for a moment to nibble at his neck. "And even though I get self-conscious in public, I still love all the attention you give me. Don't expect me to admit it again though. I still don't want you doing anything silly to me in front of other people."

Alaric chuckled.

"I don't think I have done anything too overboard yet. You are truly wonderful. A gloriously beautiful woman, with an equally beautiful personality. I can't help but want everyone else to know it too."

Angelica grabbed Alaric and rolled over on top of him, sitting up and planting both of her hands on his chest. She looked down at him, a pout trying to hide her smile.

"How about the next time you try to make me blush in public, I get to bite you and leave little teeth marks all over. And then you can buy me some flowers and a nice dinner to apologize to me for being mean."

Alaric sat up, propping himself up with one arm and using the other to brush some of Angelica's hair away from her face before resting his hand on the back of her neck.

"A few bites seem like a small price to pay for an excuse to buy you flowers and dinner. Especially if it means I also got to see your beautiful face turn red."

Angelica tried to frown as her cheeks did turn red, but Alaric grinned at her until she smiled back. She threw her arms around his neck and knocked him back down onto the bed.

"You should be nicer to me." She said, realizing that her threat had backfired.

Alaric placed his hands on her back.

"Always, my only Love. Just tell me if I ever overstep my bounds, and I will happily apologize."

Angelica grumbled, trying to think of a way she could get away with being upset at him. After a few minutes, she rolled off him and made sure she was in a position where she could look him in the eyes.

"Fine, you win. But in return for me admitting defeat, after you take your shower, you have to lay down and relax for the rest of the night. No more work today. And you have to let me kiss you, whenever I want, until you fall asleep."

Alaric chuckled again.

"I wonder if I deserve you."

Angelica smiled, giving him one more kiss before pushing him towards the edge of the bed.

"I will tell you what I believe you would tell me if I asked you that question. Whether you think you deserve me or not, I chose you."

Alaric carefully turned and stood up.

"You know me well."

Angelica grinned at him.

"I should hope so. Just be ready to accept responsibility for making me want to choose you. You are stuck with me forever."

Alaric smiled over his shoulder, heading towards the bathroom.

"Forever? For some reason, I hadn't realized how amazing spending an eternity with you will be. How exciting."

He disappeared into the bathroom and closed the door behind him.

Angelica stared at the bathroom door for a moment, feeling her cheeks burning again. She covered her face with her hands and rolled over to face the other way.

"Backfired again."

12

Chapter Twelve

Alaric stepped into a large lab filled with beakers and test tubes and innumerable vials of chemicals. The lab itself was haphazardly organized in a strange balance of ancient alchemy equipment, and cutting-edge technology. A clean new fume hood stood against one wall with an ancient stone mortar and pestle sitting next to it to seemingly emphasize the wide range of tools available.

"Is that my young Lord Alaric I hear entering my lab?" A slightly muffled voice called from the other end of the room.

"It is indeed, Master Faust." Alaric answered, closing the door quietly behind him. "Your summons said you wished to show me something?"

"Over here, my boy."

Alaric saw a scarred hand wave at him from behind a complicated set of glass tubes, most likely set up to be used for distilling several different chemicals together.

He made his way through the room, careful not to bump into any of the glassware or trip over any equipment.

As he stepped around one of the tables he saw an old man, with mostly silver hair, wearing a dirty red shirt with long sleeves and a thick leather apron. The old man had a pair of goggles sitting high up on his head out of the way while he was leaning down, looking into one of a pair of microscopes.

Alaric approached the old man and waited quietly for him to be finished.

After several moments, and a few adjustments to the focus on the microscope, the old man stepped back and waved one hand.

"Take a look there and tell me what you see."

Alaric nodded and stepped over, leaning down and placing his eyes against the microscope lens. After a few seconds, his eyes adjusted and he was able to see a multitude of blue hexagonal crystals and semi-clear filaments suspended in a faintly cloudy liquid.

"This appears to be Quintessence, synthesized into Soleum Tempus, Master Faust." Alaric straightened and looked over his shoulder at the old man.

Master Faust nodded and motioned to the second microscope.

"And what about that one?"

Alaric stepped over to the second microscope and once again placed his eyes against the lens. His eyebrows furrowed and he carefully adjusted the focus on the microscope, first one way and then the other.

"The subtle blue of this suspension would suggest the presence of Quintessence or Aether, but I don't see any crystals or Aether threads."

Master Faust nodded again.

"Then allow me to show you what it looks like when you look a bit closer."

Alaric turned and gave Master Faust a questioning look, but the old man just turned and led the way to another corner of the lab.

They walked to a darkened area, and Master Faust sat down at a cluttered computer desk. He woke up the computer screen, then opened a file and clicked on an image.

Alaric leaned down to get a closer look at the screen, bracing himself against the desk. His eyes scanned across the image and he tilted his head to one side.

"Is this a virus?" Alaric asked, looking over at Master Faust.

The old man nodded.

"Specifically, a strain of Adenovirus. Look closer."

Alaric turned back to the screen and tried to look for finer details. After a minute he leaned forward.

"Wait. The proteins on the outside of the virus seem strangely inconsistent."

"Exactly." Master Faust stated, pulling up another window with an image of a similar virus. "This is what this strain of Adenovirus should look like."

The old man leaned forward and tapped on the screen.

"As you can see, each specific protein is identical in shape and size. The one we have here has been changed."

Alaric's eyes danced back and forth between the two images.

"Indeed, but how? Did it change naturally? Or was it changed artificially? And if artificial, to what end?"

Master Faust closed the second image and zoomed in to the first one.

"We have two specific proteins on this virus and an outer structure that is not a protein. I had my suspicions about it, so I checked a few different things. The two proteins are likely meant to bind, specifically, to Human blood and Wolf blood."

Alaric looked back at Master Faust again.

"Is this...?"

Master Faust nodded.

"This is from the sample you brought me yesterday."

Alaric looked back at the screen.

"So it was used to try and bind the Human and Wolf Aspect blood together?"

Master Faust nodded again.

"It would appear so, though it goes beyond just that."

The old man stirred through some papers and eventually pulled out a single sheet and handed it to Alaric.

Alaric accepted the paper and looked at it.

"A chemical report. It looks pretty much identical to the one that the Enclave back in the U.S. had done after the first, Post-full moon, transformation occurred."

Master Faust motioned to the report.

"Based on the levels I can see on the report, everything matches what I found in solution. Everything, that is, except the levels of Quintessence."

Alaric looked over the peaks and valleys of the test.

"Did you expect to find more?"

Master Faust shook his head.

"No, quite the opposite. Based on what few crystals I could see under magnification, there should be three times less than there is."

Alaric set the paper down and looked at the old man with a confused expression.

"How does the test show that much more than you found?"

Master Faust reached out and poked the computer screen, indicating a thorn-like structure on the outside of the virus.

"That is where our missing Quintessence is. I'm not sure how they managed it. The crystalline structure of the Quintessence shouldn't be stable enough for a structure this small without breaking down, and binding it to the virus itself is also a mystery to me. But it has to be. It's the only way the levels can match."

Alaric inspected the virus once again.

"But why go to such lengths? To what end were they..." Alaric paused for a moment. "The Cursed Blood?"

Master Faust nodded.

"From what I think I can piece together, this drug was crafted to fuse the Human and Wolf blood together. Then alchemically altered silver and Quintessence crystals agitate the Cursed Blood, and Quintessence on the outside of the virus repels the Cursed Blood so it does not interfere with the Resonance of Blood. Add illicit drugs on top of that, and you then have a creature that most likely cannot be stopped or transformed back until the drug has run its course or the creature's life is ended."

Alaric shook his head.

"The potential for this is incredible. If only Elder Jayin had brought this to one of us instead of using it to experiment on the werewolves."

Master Faust nodded.

"The virus angle is one I had not yet considered. Though, technology has only relatively recently started engineering viruses for medical use. Perhaps it has reached a point that it might be a viable way to help suppress unwanted transformations for the werewolves. We might even be able to create a less harsh Soleum Tempus for ourselves. Though, without Jayin present, we will have to do all of the ground work ourselves, from scratch. Not to mention we will need to figure out how he managed to fuse the Quintessence to the virus in the first place."

Alaric nodded slowly, quickly going over the few notes and other things he had observed at Elder Jayin's estate. Then a frown slowly grew on his face and he looked down at his own hand.

"It may have been sorcery."

Master Faust looked up at Alaric.

"That would be a problem. Is there a reasonable way we could test that?"

Alaric pushed himself away from the desk.

"Do you still have some of the sample left that was not used up?"

Master Faust stood up and walked back across the room to the two microscopes, Alaric in tow. He picked up a foam block that was full of holes that had several plastic tubes resting in them and pulled one out that was about half full of light blue liquid.

"This is what was left after I separated it for the tests." Master Faust said, holding the tube out to Alaric.

Alaric carefully took the tube and placed it between his thumb and forefinger. He rolled it back and forth between his fingers for a moment until it took on a subtle glow. After a few seconds, he placed it in the palm of his other hand and held it out to Master Faust, the glow fading away.

"Run the same tests on this sample, and look at it under a microscope. If the structures on the virus were Quintessence, held together by sorcery, they should have fallen apart now. If they are somehow still whole and attached, then they must have been attached some other way."

Master Faust took the tube with a nod.

"Sorcery certainly has its uses. Though I hope to find this was accomplished through Alchemy or some such. Having to delve into an entirely new discipline will only monopolize more of your precious time, my boy."

Alaric chuckled.

"Indeed. I already have so much to do, I hope I am wrong in assuming this is sorcery."

Alaric heard a subtle creak across the room, and Master Faust tried to turn and look over his equipment.

"Who is it? What do you need?"

"I was asked to seek out Lord Alaric. Elder Amalia is asking for him urgently and Lord Angelica said he could be found here." The voice was slightly muted, clearly spoken by someone who had chosen not to step into the room.

Alaric frowned.

"I am here. Please tell Elder Amalia I am on my way, thank you."

"Very well." The voice responded, and then the door clicked shut again.

Master Faust grumbled.

"Well, better go see what our Lady wants. She has seemed to be in an unpleasant mood for the past several days."

Alaric half bowed to Master Faust.

"That may be my doing, in part. My apologies, Master Faust. I will try to appease her. Please keep me apprised as to how your tests go."

Master Faust patted Alaric's shoulder.

"Of course, my boy. Go take care of the politicians and leave the science to me."

* * *

Alaric frowned as he approached Elder Amalia's room. Two guards were posted outside, and several others were hurrying in and out of the room, almost in a panic.

Alaric nodded to the two guards outside and slipped into the room. Inside he found Amalia giving directions to several guards. He also noticed Angelica standing against one wall with her arms folded over her chest, clearly unhappy.

"Ensure the Elders remain in their rooms. Each is to have two guards at all times. There needs to be patrols throughout the Hive every five minutes. No less than six guards per patrol at any time until further notice."

Amalia noticed Alaric enter and waved off the other guards.

"The rest of you must report to Elder Mihail for assignments in guarding the drone segments of the Hive. Remain vigilant."

The guards all bowed and rushed from the room. Alaric waited for them all to leave, then closed the door behind them and quickly walked over to Amalia.

"What is going on? Has something happened?"

Amalia nodded with a frown. Not a frown of anger or frustration, but one of pain and profound sadness.

"The guards protecting the pass to The Library were attacked. Three are severely injured and will need blood to survive... Two of them are already dead."

Alaric felt a jolt shoot through him, a sharp pain in his chest followed by a flame of anger.

"Was it sorcery?"

Amalia nodded slowly, a tear starting to roll down her cheek.

Alaric growled and turned on his heels, not waiting for Amalia to speak.

"Keep everyone away from The Library until my return."

He reached the door and grasped the handle, a second hand reaching out and touching his.

"I am coming with you."

Alaric looked at Angelica out of the corner of his eye and saw an adamant expression of determination on her face. She was not asking.

Alaric sighed, wrangling his emotions so as not to take his frustrations out on anyone undeserving.

"Stay behind me. Don't face him directly on your own."

Angelica nodded.

Alaric turned the handle and they both rushed from the room. They quickly moved through the tunnels of the Hive, dodging around frantic guards who were running from one place to another.

Alaric could smell something akin to sulfur as they approached the large natural cave opening that would lead them out into the open mountains. As they rounded the corner, he could see the source of the smell. The place where the guards had been attacked.

Alaric took Angelica's hand, pulling her forward, not allowing her even a moment to pause and look at the scorch marks on the stone floor and walls.

They hurried out into the night air, following the narrow stone pass that gradually widened until it opened up into a long valley with tall mountains on either side.

The valley itself was covered in little other than grass and dirt, the grass itself gradually growing thinner and more sickly as it approached the cliffs at the other end of the valley.

Alaric's eyes scanned the valley floor, slowing down.

"What's wrong?" Angelica asked quietly, also sweeping the area with her eyes.

Alaric frowned.

"There is something here. Something infused with magic."

He slowed further and then came to a stop entirely. They waited several moments, carefully watching their surroundings, and then Angelica noticed a pair of glowing yellow eyes.

"There are more of them." Alaric warned quietly.

Angelica looked around and spotted another pair of eyes, then another, and another. The longer they waited, the more eyes opened and watched them, until they were almost entirely surrounded by a sea of glowing eyes.

Eventually, Angelica spotted a pair of eyes near enough to see what they belonged to. It was a small, almost human-like figure, seemingly formed out of clay.

"Golems. I thought it was suspicious that this sorcerer was able to find his way to The Library so quickly. Elder Jayin must have been smuggling him in at regular intervals. There is no way he made this many golems in so short a period of time. We'll have to destroy them now, or they will just ambush us from behind when we try to face the sorcerer."

Angelica nudged Alaric forward.

"You go on ahead. I'll take care of these. You save your strength for fighting the one who conjured them."

Alaric looked over his shoulder.

"Are you certain?"

Angelica nodded, her hair beginning to glow and lift from her shoulders.

"Positive. Let me guard your back. Besides," She grinned bitterly. "I think I am feeling some aggression that I really should work out."

Alaric smirked, just as bitterly.

"That's my Angie. I'm counting on you."

As if by some unseen signal, they both vanished. An enormous burst of flame erupted into the sky as Angelica struck the nearest golem, reducing it to dust.

Alaric looked back once, having cleared the area surrounded by the golems, then hurried forward.

He ran along the valley until he saw a tall, flat cliff at the opposite end. He slowed as he approached, noticing runes glowing brightly in a large arch along the cliff face.

As he got closer he started to feel magic being used and, soon after, noticed a bright green aura shining from the base of the cliffs.

Alaric slowed to a walk and then came to a stop once he could clearly see the man, with his arms outstretched, standing at the center of the aura.

He was a middle-aged man with tan skin. He had very short black hair on his head, but a long beard on his face. He wore simple brown robes, with a leather belt and several pouches tied around his waist.

"It is in your best interest not to open that place." Alaric called out.

The bright green aura faded away, and the sorcerer lowered his arms.

"And it is in yours not to interrupt me, vampire."

13

Chapter Thirteen

Alaric stood, straight-backed and proud.

"Do you even understand what you are trying to do? Did Jayin ever explain what would happen to you if you entered The Library?"

The sorcerer turned to face Alaric.

"Why should I care about disease? Be it the Spanish Flu or the Black Death. Even if it were to call down the twelve plagues of Egypt, it is no business of mine if the world falls to pieces while I take what I deserve. And if I happen across this 'Origin Cursebearer' and gain Cursed Blood, all the better. The long life of the vampires suits me well."

Alaric shook his head.

"Our long life is granted by our Pact with The Fey. The Cursed Blood is no path to immortality, it can only destroy. You would be better off seeking a Pact of your own, or divine relics and blessings. Even Necromancy is a better choice than what you are attempting. At least that will not cost you your sorcery."

The sorcerer smirked.

"You vampires cannot keep the infinite knowledge of The Library hidden for yourselves. I will bring about a new golden age for this world, with myself as its god. If I must sacrifice most of the world to achieve it, then I will gladly pay that price. After all, the people should be grateful to sacrifice themselves for the sake of their god."

Alaric frowned deeply.

"Even we vampires are not so self-assured as to blaspheme so readily. The great spirits and the divines notwithstanding, attempting any such thing would turn the world herself against you. And all the power of all the sorcerers in the world could not protect you from her fiery wrath."

The sorcerer continued to smirk.

"Old wives tales designed to scare young sorcerers at The Academy won't sway me. You will have to try much harder than that, vampire. And threats will do you no good either. I have seen the strength of your kind. You are nothing before the power of my sorcery."

Alaric took a slow breath, forcing the fires of anger back down into his chest.

"You have seen nothing, sorcerer. Those you attacked on your way here were caught by surprise. And Jayin was, by far, the weakest of our Elders. He ruled only through his Command. Even the enforcers and guards could have defeated him in direct combat. And I doubt you have yet to experience a vampire calling upon their element."

The sorcerer chuckled.

"You must think quite highly of yourself, vampire. You talk awfully big for someone who had to sneak all over Europe to even dare visit the Elder you are calling weak. You didn't even manage to get rid of Jayin. I can still sense he is alive, so your words ring hollow."

Alaric shook his head.

"I would have loved nothing more than to take Jayin apart, piece by piece, but I had already promised him to another. He yet lives, this is true, but I assure you he will continue to live his very long life regretting the fact that I did not end him with my own hand. Farsight can show you only so much and you are too much of a fool to understand why you can only sense his life, and not see it."

The sorcerer frowned.

"I think you are the only person who has ever dared call me a fool. Of course, if you knew who you were talking to, perhaps you wouldn't have. I suppose I should simply chalk that up to ignorance on your part.

Or maybe that high and mighty attitude you vampires all seem to carry so proudly, as if it were a badge of honor."

Alaric's eyes flashed for a moment.

"You will find that experience and wisdom are, quite often, mistaken for false pride. Personally, I do not like to take any sort of pride in myself, going so far as to hide any skill or knowledge I have so that I may appear like no more than the average man. I can sense that the cards you drew at The Academy are above the average, but your strength is nowhere near enough to face me. The mere fact that you cannot sense it yourself, is proof of that. I must assure you, no matter how long you lived or traveled, you would never face a vampire more powerful than me."

The sorcerer growled.

"I grow tired of your self-righteous prattling. I have delayed my ascension long enough. Your death, self-proclaimed greatest of vampires, will serve as a warning to the others to never rebel against their new god again."

The sorcerer raised his arm, his green aura returning like a newly kindled fire. Power quickly gathered in his open hand, creating a ball of crackling energy.

With a flick of his wrist, the energy almost instantly traveled the distance between him and Alaric. It struck with enough force to shake the ground around them, creating a fiery explosion that lit up the mountains and valley.

The sorcerer smirked and then turned around to face the runes on the cliffs again.

"You have never faced an opponent strong enough to challenge you before, have you?"

The sorcerer spun around in alarm as Alaric spoke.

Alaric stood, one hand raised, surrounded by a dense golden aura that protected his body like armor.

"Only a fool turns his back on an enemy before verifying, with their own eyes, that they have been defeated."

The sorcerer smirked again, though it was clear that much of his previous confidence was gone.

"I'm surprised. I didn't think I would need to go all out, so I held back. Apparently, that was a mistake."

Alaric lowered his hand.

"You have merely never faced anyone who was above average before. Or even one that was close to you in power. You don't understand what it means to face an equal, let alone someone who is stronger."

The sorcerer frowned for a moment, clearly thinking that it might be possible that Alaric could be as strong as him. Then he smirked again.

"Well, I wish I had the time to face you in a proper battle. It might be interesting to have a slight challenge for once. But I have things to do, and you are getting in my way."

He reached into one of the pouches at his side and pulled out a translucent blue crystal.

Alaric frowned.

"Do not do anything foolish. Channeling your power through that crystal will make it too strong for you to control. Not only could you destroy yourself in the process, but you could break the seals on The Library and destroy the doors behind them at the same time."

"All the better. I destroy you, and get into The Library, in one fell blow."

Alaric shook his head, his fierce eyes piercing through the other sorcerer.

"Even if it would allow you to defeat me, which it will not, if the doors are broken down and not remade this world will begin to unravel. As you are also of this world, that means you will also be unmade and cease to exist. The Library is a dangerous place that holds things beyond mortal comprehension. It is not some simple pile of books for you to read through."

The sorcerer growled, raising his hand above his head.

"You will not keep me from my destiny!"

As the sorcerer yelled he crushed the crystal and, for a moment, everything was silent. Then a deafening roar echoed through the mountains as the sorcerer's aura swelled explosively outward, blue now mixing with the green to create a colossal, multicolored, dancing flame. There was a cracking sound, and the runes on the cliffside behind the sorcerer began to glow even more brightly.

Alaric growled angrily, shading his eyes with one hand.

"Fine. Just remember, you forced my hand. Do not spend what little time you have left regretting it."

Alaric held his arms out to either side, palms facing up, and concentrated his power in his chest. In a flash of light, like the first moment of the morning sun rising above the horizon, Alaric was engulfed in a golden flame that lit up the valley around them as bright as day. The golden flames blazed outward and pressed against the blue and green flames of the enemy sorcerer and threatened to smother them.

"I will not be broken!" The sorcerer screamed over the roar of the flames around them.

Hollow chanting filled the air, reaching the heart and mind, even through the roaring sounds of the clashing auras. Power started to gather into a bright sphere at the center of the blue and green flames.

Alaric took a deep breath, his eyes turning a solid metallic gold. He raised one hand, directing his focus towards the sorcerer, and clamped it tightly shut.

"Be silenced."

The simple words caused the golden flames to crash over the sorcerer in a swirling maelstrom, snuffing out his blue and green flames in an instant. The bright orb at the center of the flames shattered like a glass ornament and was scattered, as if by a powerful wind.

An almost inhuman shriek filled the air for several seconds before the golden flames burned out and left everything dark and quiet once again.

The sorcerer lay face down, his clothes and body singed by the pure magical energy that had just washed over him.

Alaric spared him barely a glance before walking towards the cliffs.

"I thought only a fool turns his back on an enemy before verifying he is defeated!" The sorcerer yelled, leaping at Alaric with a silver-bladed knife in his hand.

Alaric ignored him and continued walking, a flash of red descending from the sky behind them and striking the sorcerer from above.

In a fraction of a second, the sorcerer found himself held by the throat, his feet dangling above the ground, by a woman with weightless glowing red hair. A scowl, and a flame deep within her eyes, caused him to shake with a wave of fear.

He stabbed at her with his silver knife and she batted it aside, sending the knife flying and shattering the bones in his hand and forearm with the force of her blow.

"I want, so very badly, to bite you and drain you of every last drop of blood." She said, with an almost feral growl. "But that would be too kind a death for one who has slain my kin, and attacked My Love."

She pulled him closer until her mouth was near his ear and he had begun to whimper. She opened her mouth, allowing a soft sigh to escape her before she whispered,

"And so, instead, you will burn."

In an instant, they were both engulfed in bright red flames.

The sorcerer shrieked in panic and agony as his hair and skin began to burn.

Angelica stood amidst the flames, fire flowing all around her in a whirlwind of searing heat. She allowed the sorcerer to scream and suffer for several long seconds, struggling to escape her grasp. Then she lifted her chin slightly and her eyes turned a fiery red. The flames around her roared to life, and grew white-hot, stripping the dirt and grass from the ground at her feet all the way down to the bare stone beneath.

The sorcerer shrieked and was suddenly reduced to ash, his remains scattering to the winds while his last scream still echoed in the valley.

The flames died away, leaving Angelica standing on a patch of glowing rock, waves of heat rising from the ground around her.

She turned and walked towards the cliffs, her hair returning to normal and falling around her shoulders. She carefully followed where Alaric had gone until she reached the cliffs and stood beside him.

She could see several large cracks running up the stone cliff face, and the glowing runes were very slowly dissolving.

"Were we too late?" She asked, flinching as a cracking sound caused one of the cracks to grow.

Alaric shook his head.

"No, he used the entire piece of Quintessence we were missing all at once. There was no way for him to control that much power, and it damaged the seal and the door to The Library."

Alaric's eyes ran over the cliff and then he sighed in exasperation.

"With this much damage, I am going to have to go inside to ensure the Origin Cursebearer did not wake. If he did, he will have to be put to sleep again before we can reseal The Library and repair the doors. I only hope the doors were not damaged to the point that they will release an epidemic."

Angelica frowned, trying to think of a way she could help.

"Perhaps you are fortunate, then, that I have arrived when I have." A voice called out.

They both turned and found a woman approaching them. She had dark skin and wore long, loose clothing. She had long dark hair, with a few strands of gray beginning to show through, and had a small round gemstone in the center of her forehead.

Alaric bowed, and Angelica quickly followed his example.

"Master Ahanna, it is good to see you again. You are truly a sight for sore eyes."

Master Ahanna bowed in return.

"Master Alaric. I heard from your young leader what was happening, and felt your power radiating across the mountains. Is the danger passed?"

Alaric nodded.

"The immediate danger, yes. The sorcerer is no more. However, now we must deal with the dangers of The Library itself."

Master Ahanna approached the runes.

"Is this the place you spoke of to me?"

Alaric nodded.

"It is."

She placed her hand on the stone and closed her eyes for several seconds.

"I see. The seal became overcharged and is burning away, and the barrier between us and the place beyond is also damaged. I sense something deep and unsettling within. Something with a truly ravenous hunger."

Alaric nodded again.

"There are things beyond the barrier that must be kept inside. Not least of which is the one that passed the Curse into our ancestor's blood. I was hoping just to remake the seals, but I am afraid I will have to venture within to ensure the Cursebearer is still held in sleep. If he has awakened, it will be far more difficult to keep the effects of The Library in check. Would you be so kind, Master Ahanna, as to keep vigil here to ensure the seal does not break until I can return?"

"You haven't much time. Maybe a matter of hours, at best, before the whole seal breaks apart. But I will do as much as I can."

Alaric nodded once more.

"I understand. But it is important that this be done. If, by some chance, I have not been able to return before the seal breaks, please reforge it with me inside."

"No, Alaric." Angelica nervously grabbed hold of Alaric's coat.

Alaric put his hand over hers.

"I have to do this, Angie. There is no other way. Please, wait for me here. And if I must be trapped inside, just know our bond reaches across all of time. I will still be in your heart. No matter what happens, I will always return to you."

Angelica frowned, feeling tears in her eyes. She threw her arms around him and squeezed him tightly. After a few seconds, she quickly let go and turned away.

"Go quickly. Please, while I can still let you go."

Alaric smiled sadly and turned, placing one hand on the cliff side. After a moment, a soft light enveloped him and he was gone.

Angelica sniffled and tried to wipe the tears out of her eyes. She felt a warm hand on her shoulder and remembered that Master Ahanna was still there.

"Oh, I'm sorry. I forgot to properly introduce myself. I am Angelica." Angelica quickly turned and bowed.

"Ahanna." The master sorcerer paused for a moment. "You care greatly for him."

Angelica smiled, doing her best not to cry.

"We are married, so it would be a bit too late now if I didn't."

Master Ahanna smiled in return.

"Do not be worried. Have faith that he will return to us quickly."

Angelica sniffled again, wishing she had a tissue to wipe her nose with.

"Thank you. I'm sorry, I'm not exactly handling this very well."

Master Ahanna nodded.

"That is quite understandable."

Master Ahanna paused for a few more moments and then spoke again.

"I assume you were the one who left the shattered remains of the golems at the entrance to the valley? I must say, Master Alaric was quite right about you."

Angelica blinked a few times.

"He was?"

Master Ahanna nodded, turning back to face the cliff.

"He loves to speak of you whenever he gets the chance. He said you were a beautiful, resilient, reliable woman. Powerful, skilled, with an innocent and soft heart beneath everything else. Someone capable of great empathy, and great strength. I can see now that there was little exaggeration in his claims."

Angelica felt tears in her eyes again and her cheeks were burning.

"I have to bite him when he gets back."

14

Chapter Fourteen

Alaric stood quietly, taking a few moments to get his bearings. He was standing in a small opening between two bookshelves. In front of him, just to his right next to the bookshelf, was a small table loaded with stacks of books. A small wooden chair was tucked neatly beneath the table. The bookshelves extended to either side for what seemed to be around a hundred feet.

Alaric looked up and found that the bookshelves reached up until they disappeared into the shadows, and there was no sign of a ceiling at all.

As Alaric looked back down he could see a long hall stretching out before him, made by the gaps between the bookshelves. He walked forward until he reached the next shelf.

In front of him, just to his right next to the bookshelf, was a small table loaded with stacks of books.

Alaric paused, glancing back over his shoulder. The table he had just passed was still there, but the one before him looked identical down to the last detail. Even the books stacked on the table were the same books in the same positions.

Alaric looked at the shelves to see if they were the same as well, but he found he was unable to focus on the books and was not able to tell if they were the same or not.

Alaric closed his eyes for a moment, reaching out with his senses, but was unpleasantly surprised to find that he could not sense anything at all around him, aside from a vague sense of hunger. It was as if he was standing in the vacuum of space, out of touch with everything else in the universe.

Alaric opened his eyes, and once again found himself standing in the small opening between the bookshelves. He stood for several more moments, then started walking.

Alaric passed shelf after shelf after shelf, each one filled with books he could not look at. Beside each shelf, as he passed each opening, was an identical table stacked with identical books.

Alaric continued walking, counting the rows he passed. Ten, twenty, fifty, a hundred. No matter how many shelves and tables he passed, nothing changed. The table remained the same. The books were always stacked the same way, in the same order. The small wooden chair always tucked neatly underneath. Nothing ever changed.

Until it did.

Alaric passed the one hundred and forty-second shelf and immediately noticed that the small wooden chair was slightly further back than it had been on the previous table.

He kept walking.

Three more rows and the chair had moved again.

Five more rows and the chair had turned slightly.

Four more rows and now the chair was facing away from the table.

Alaric continued walking for another twenty rows without any change, and then he passed one final shelf and found someone sitting in the chair.

The man's head was tilted forward against his chest. He had jet-black hair and wore a full set of bright red robes. He sat quietly, his hands resting gently in his lap, his eyes closed.

Alaric stopped, turning carefully to face the man.

"Elder Olbrecht?"

The man stirred slightly.

"A voice?" He grumbled. "How long has it been since I heard a voice? Could I have heard anything at all?"

Alaric frowned.

"Can you hear me, Elder?"

The man moved again, trying to lift his head.

"A familiar voice? I know this person... I think?"

The man slowly managed to raise his head and his eyes fluttered open.

"Young Alaric? Is that you? It is difficult to focus."

Alaric nodded carefully.

"It is I, Elder Olbrecht. I am surprised to see you. I was under the impression that the curse had finally taken your life."

The man blinked a few times, slowly processing what had been said.

"Yes, that is right, I am Olbrecht Amaison. I was with Janison and Cennia. We found what we were looking for."

"Can you not remember, Elder?" Alaric asked.

The man looked up at Alaric.

"Remember? Elder? Young Alaric... that is right... grandchild of Cennia. You served with strength of heart. Yes, it... it seems the fog is thinning."

The man blinked a few more times and looked around.

"Oh, we are within The Library. You should not be here, young one."

Alaric nodded.

"I am sorry, Elder, I had not wished to intrude here. But the seal and the doors were damaged. I had to be certain that the Cursebearer was not awakened by it."

The man looked around a bit more and then back at Alaric.

"The Cursebearer?" A light seemed to turn on in the man's eyes. "Oh, I remember now. I am sorry, young one, for the confusion. Creating a corporeal form is difficult. I am not Olbrecht Amaison. Not in a true sense, anyway. You were correct. The touch of the void took that person's life some time ago. I am a mere reflection of his memories and experiences."

Alaric nodded, inspecting the man but seeing nothing that would have identified him as anything but Elder Olbrecht.

"I see. That being the case, who created the reflection? And for what purpose?"

The man nodded.

"Indeed. I am a fragment of the one who watches over this place. My name cannot be spoken by human tongues, so you may refer to me as you already know me. As Cursebearer."

Alaric frowned.

"You are the Cursebearer? So you have awakened then."

The Cursebearer shook his head.

"No, I still slumber. Though I never truly sleep. At least, not in the same sense as mortal beings do. I merely sensed that you had entered my domain, and chose this form to commune with you."

Alaric clasped his hands behind his back.

"If that is so, then why did you feel the need to commune with me?"

The Cursebearer carefully reached up, looking curiously at his hand for a moment and then scratching his chin.

"The Library is a place not meant to be traversed by mortal minds. It is a place outside of your world but not wholly separated from it. It is pressed, precariously, between the physical world and The Void. I am a being born of the black thoughts within The Void. Incomprehensible to most all with physical form. Contact with me, and by extension The Void itself, is what caused the condition you call a Curse."

Alaric felt his blood racing in his body as he absorbed this information.

"I see. That is something we had never realized before about ourselves. Appreciative as I am about receiving this information, however, why do you feel the need to tell me this?"

The Cursebearer motioned to the shelves around him.

"I want to try and be as clear as I can. What has happened to you, your ancestors and your descendants, was not due to malice. Merely the chain of events caused by coming into contact with The Void. This is important for you to understand."

Alaric nodded once.

"I believe I understand what you are saying, but the purpose behind this necessity for understanding is what still eludes me."

The Cursebearer straightened in his chair.

"Of course, forgive me. I have not yet spoken on what is to come. I forget that time, for mortals, is a mostly linear experience. Only a precious few can stand on the bank of the river and see beyond their own moments."

Alaric frowned.

"I do not find it wise to peer into the future often."

The Cursebearer nodded.

"Knowing what is to come can be a dreadful, and misleading, thing. However, I was tasked to speak of it. To speak so that the world may be ready."

Alaric's frown deepened.

"Who would be able to task one such as yourself with anything? And what portent is so dire that the world must be warned of its coming?"

The Cursebearer nodded again, waving one hand slowly.

"He is one beyond even my comprehension. His voice commanded, and I knew I must obey. He is in your world as we speak, keeping watch. A Guardian of great power and knowledge. He knew you would come here eventually. You will meet him in time, and you will know him when you do. As for what must be brought to light... The barrier between worlds has grown thin. The Void will try to enter your world and devour it. It cannot act on its own, only through others. Only through those already within the world, may it find a way to pierce through the veil. You must be vigilant in keeping these others from acting. Lest your world unravel before its time."

Alaric felt tension growing in his chest and stomach.

"I see. That is, indeed, cause for great concern. If this is the case, then I sincerely express my appreciation to you for bringing it to my attention."

The Cursebearer nodded once and waved towards the shelves again.

"I did as I was bidden, and as I was encouraged to do. I have very little by way of a physical form. I am more a collection of thoughts and ideas and memories. When those who were tainted by the touch of The Void passed on, their hearts and minds were imprinted on me as well. They all became one with me. The ones you called Elder wished to speak with you. Therefore, in part, so did I."

Alaric thought over this for a few moments and then bowed.

"Thank you for speaking with me. I will take what you have said to heart, and pass it along to those I believe can help."

The Cursebearer nodded again, this time with a semblance of a smile on his face.

"Do be careful not to let anyone else enter this place again. It is far too dangerous for mortal kind, and disrupts my Library of Thought. Also, the ones who were known as Olbrecht and Cennia wish for you to tell their children that they are proud of the care they have taken to protect everything they have been a part of."

Alaric straightened with a nod.

"I will do my best to convey their feelings."

The Cursebearer waved one hand, and Alaric felt an uncomfortable feeling in the pit of his stomach.

"Very well, then I will dismiss you from this place. Goodbye, young Alaric."

The Cursebearer began to turn black and fade away. As he did, the Library also faded and Alaric felt as if someone was pulling him backwards with a rope that was tied around his spine.

Alaric stumbled back, with a queasy feeling in his stomach, and felt a pair of hands reach out and grab his shoulders.

"Are you alright, Alaric? My Love?"

Alaric smiled as he felt the cool mountain air blow across his face. He steadied himself and then turned to face Angelica.

"I am well, Angie. Thank you." He placed one hand on her shoulder, and one on her cheek, and then kissed her forehead. "Please take a step back. Master Ahanna and I must repair the door and make a temporary seal to hold until Master Takanashi can arrive."

Angelica accepted Alaric's kiss, then put her arms around him and squeezed him for a moment before taking a few steps back.

Alaric smiled at her again and then turned to Master Ahanna.

"Master Ahanna, would you please do me the honor of allowing me to aid you in repairing the seal?"

Master Ahanna nodded.

"If you will do me the honor of aiding me in doing so, Master Alaric."

Alaric nodded in return and they both turned and faced the cliffs.

They raised their arms out at shoulder level, their fingertips nearly touching, and a subtle golden aura settled around them. The golden aura grew brighter, and larger, and brighter still until they had both been enveloped in a golden flame so bright that even their silhouettes were barely visible within.

As the great golden flame expanded and grew, Angelica was forced to take another step back and turn away to protect her eyes. The entire valley before her was brightly lit as if the sun itself was rising behind her.

She stood silently, feeling the weight of the magic being cast pressing against her back. She watched the flickering light reflecting off the surrounding mountains, wishing she could turn around and see what was happening.

After several minutes it suddenly felt like the air had grown cleaner, and the weight behind Angelica began to fade along with the golden light. After a few more moments, she felt it was safe to look and turned back around.

The cracks in the cliffs had disappeared and there were new glowing runes spreading out along the surface from a central point above their heads.

"That shall be good enough." Master Ahanna said, lowering her arms. "At least until Master Takanashi and I can plan out a more permanent solution."

Alaric turned and bowed to Master Ahanna.

"Thank you, once again, for your help."

Master Ahanna nodded and smiled gently.

"Of course, Master Alaric. I don't believe a single one of us would ever ignore a call for aid from you. We all know you would do the same for us."

Alaric smiled back.

"I appreciate your aid nonetheless."

Alaric turned, and Angelica was already throwing herself into his arms. She reached over and started chewing on the side of his neck, though she was careful not to break skin.

"You have been talking to people about me again, haven't you?" Angelica accused him between bites.

Alaric chuckled, turning his head to kiss her neck while she nibbled on him.

"I see Master Ahanna has told on me." He said.

Master Ahanna did her best to cover her smile with one hand and began walking back across the valley to leave the two to themselves.

Angelica grumbled.

"You made me cry in front of her too, and she was super nice about it, and that just made it worse."

Alaric could feel Angelica's face heating up and laughed softly.

"I am sorry I had to leave you here on your own, My Dearest Love. I especially didn't want to make you cry. Please forgive me."

Angelica sighed and laid her head on Alaric's shoulder.

"I know, My Love. I just couldn't bear the thought of even the slightest chance that you would not return."

Alaric took a half step back and lifted Angelica's chin. He kissed her gently and then placed his forehead against hers.

"I will never leave you alone. Even if we are separated, at any point in time, I will return to you. Even if I have to take the world apart and put it back together again to reach you, I will. Nothing in this world, or any other, will keep me from you."

Angelica smiled, allowing a few tears to roll down her cheeks.

"I will hold you to that, My Love."

She kissed him back and then placed her face against his chest.

"Thank you." She whispered, and Alaric could tell she was trying to hide her tears from him now.

Alaric rested his chin on her head and held her quietly. He waited for several minutes, until she stopped sniffling, before speaking again.

"Are you ready to go back?"

Angelica shook her head, keeping her face pressed firmly against his chest.

"Do we have to?"

Alaric chuckled.

"I am afraid so. There are things I need to convey to Elder Amalia, and the sun will be rising soon." He bowed his head next hers and his voice lowered to a whisper. "But, once I am done with the Elder, I have nothing else I need to do until after Master Takanashi arrives tomorrow. We can spend all day alone in our room. If you would like."

He felt Angelica smile and she rubbed her cheek against his.

"That would be nice."

Alaric kissed her cheek and stepped back, holding his hand out to her.

"Then shall we go back?"

Angelica grinned, taking hold of his hand with one of hers and rubbing her eyes with the other.

"As long as you promise not to let go of my hand until we get back to our room."

Alaric smiled, squeezing her hand and leading the way back.

"I swear I will not let loose your hand until I have safely escorted you to our room, my lady. After which I will speak with our Elder and then return to you forthwith."

Angelica giggled, leaning against Alaric's arm.

"Lead on then, good knight."

15

Chapter Fifteen

Alaric leaned carefully against a wall outside Amalia's room, waiting patiently for her to return from the council room.

The halls of the Hive were quiet and still. Not surprising to Alaric, considering the sun had risen not long ago. He decided to close his eyes and simply waited.

"Should you not be sleeping in your own room?" A voice asked.

Alaric opened his eyes and found Amalia standing next to him in her red council robes.

"Quiet as ever I see, Elder. I would like nothing more than to be laying in my bed just now, but there are things I must discuss with you before I may do so."

Amalia sighed tiredly and opened her door.

"I see. Very well. Come in. You may sit while I change into something more comfortable."

Alaric followed her into the room and looked around to find a seat. There were several tables, potted plants, and a few chairs pushed up against the walls. Alaric assumed everything had been pushed aside to make room for the guards to meet with Amalia the night before.

He took a moment to pull a chair away from the wall, then found a large armchair which he also pulled out. He sat in the first chair, feeling some of his muscles becoming sore from the effort of the day as he did.

He waited several minutes before Amalia came out of the secluded bedroom, now wearing a pair of red silk pajamas. She had pulled her long hair out of its tight bun and it now laid messily around her back and shoulders.

She yawned widely as she approached, slowly noticing the chairs Alaric had moved. She walked over and climbed up into the large armchair, sliding all the way to the back of the chair and letting her feet dangle off the front.

"My apologies for the state of my room. I have yet to have the time to set it to rights."

Alaric smiled.

"There is no need for concern, Elder, I understand."

Amalia frowned, putting her hands in her lap.

"Please, Alaric, just for today, don't call me Elder."

Alaric continued to smile, though it did take on a sad tone.

"Very well, Amalia. Just for today."

Amalia nodded, a shuddering sigh escaping her lips.

"Was The Library safe? The magic you used was so heavy that even those of us not sensitive to sorcery could feel it."

Alaric leaned back in his own chair.

"I was able to stop the sorcerer from opening it, but he used the missing Quintessence to try anyway. He caused some damage to the seal and the doors, but Master Ahanna arrived in time to help me repair the damage."

Amalia nodded.

"That is good. I spoke with her but briefly. She seemed a kind soul. I shall be interested in speaking with her more, time permitting."

Alaric smiled again.

"Master Ahanna has always been kind. She is intelligent and inquisitive as well, so I am certain she would also be interested in a conversation with you, if the both of you can find the time."

Amalia laid her head back against her chair, thinking quietly.

Alaric left her to her thoughts for a moment before speaking.

"Were we able to get blood donated to save the injured guards?" Amalia nodded.

"Yes, fortunately. They should recover in a day or two. Were it that we could have saved all of them."

Alaric smiled sadly but shook his head.

"Do not let yourself carry the guilt for their loss, Amalia. No one would have expected the sorcerer to make a move so quickly. We could not have been prepared for what happened."

Amalia frowned but kept her head tilted back and didn't look at Alaric.

"Let me feel guilty. I felt confident in the strength of the Hive. Had you not been here, The Library would have been taken, and there is no telling what disaster may have befallen us. I must give Angelica my thanks for being reckless and forcing you to come to us sooner than you had planned."

Alaric did his best not to chuckle.

"The two of you both like to feel more guilt than is due. Aside from our losses, things went as well as we could likely have hoped. The doors to The Library were damaged, and so I was forced to risk entering to ensure the Cursebearer's slumber had not been disturbed. But I learned several things that we would not have known otherwise, so that ended up being beneficial to us. And because the sorcerer acted so hastily, we were able to find and deal with him quickly. His use of the Quintessence was unfortunate, but it also allowed us to account for everything we were missing. We can at least be assured now that there is no more that can be used to cause harm to our cousins, the werewolves."

Amalia nodded, though her frown did become angrier.

"I hope you at least made him suffer for what he did."

Alaric smirked bitterly.

"I broke his pride, and his confidence in his own abilities. As for suffering, Angie got her hands on him in the end. It sounded quite painful."

Amalia finally tilted her head forward again and looked at Alaric. Her frown slowly disappeared, but she didn't appear any happier.

"Once again, I will have to tender my thanks to Angelica. I guess my thirst for blood will have to be considered sated. What, then, is this you said about entering The Library?"

Alaric leaned forward and rested his elbows on his knees.

"With the damage to the seal and doors, I was concerned that the Origin Cursebearer may have been awakened from his slumber. I entered, leaving Angelica and Master Ahanna outside to ensure the seal would not break, and looked through The Library for signs that the Cursebearer had awakened. I was prepared to do what I could to return him to his slumber if that was the case."

Amalia nodded.

"And what did you find?"

Alaric motioned with one hand.

"The Cursebearer."

Amalia visibly stiffened. Alaric nodded.

"He had not been fully awakened, but part of him was aware of my presence. He chose to take a physical form to speak to me."

Amalia shook herself.

"But why would he do that? Did he do anything to you?"

Alaric shook his head.

"I am well. We stayed apart and never made contact. He said he wanted to speak with me and ensure that we understood some things about the world and ourselves. That he, himself, was not malevolent. Merely dangerous for mortals to interact with."

Amalia scrunched her nose.

"That is hard to believe."

Alaric nodded with a smile.

"I understand. I was also hesitant to believe as much. But he was open with me and answered my questions directly. I don't believe he has any reason to lie, and other things he spoke of make me believe he really was being helpful. At least, what he interprets to be helpful."

Amalia grumbled, shifting in her chair to try and get more comfortable.

"If he isn't a malevolent being, then what is he? Why did he curse us?"

Alaric rubbed his face, trying to think of a way to put his thoughts into words.

"What do you know of our world and what lies beyond?"

Amalia scratched her head.

"Well, our world is like a living thing. It has its own life force. I know we are attached to several other realms, like the Fey Wilds and the Spirit World. Is there much else to know?"

Alaric shook his head, an unamused laugh escaping him.

"Much more. But the most important point for this conversation is what lies between us and the other realms."

"Between?" Amalia tried to sit up straighter.

Alaric nodded.

"Yes. The realms aren't pressed against each other, there is space between them. That is why it can be so difficult to get from one realm to another, and often takes powerful sorcery or other magic to achieve."

Amalia nodded.

"Okay, that makes sense. So what is important about this space? What is there?"

Alaric half smiled.

"Nothing. Absolute nothingness. A nothingness so profound and hungry that any physical world or entity that is exposed to it is devoured. Unraveled down to its very core until it simply ceases to exist. The only thing that survives are fragments of thought and memory. Only a thin layer of protection keeps the realms from being devoured by this Void."

Amalia started to frown again.

"What does this have to do with the Cursebearer?"

Alaric sat back in his chair, stretching his back slightly.

"The Library is a realm outside of our own. Stuck in the thin layer between our world and The Void. The entity we know of as the Origin

Cursebearer was created of The Void. A collection of the fragments of thought and memory that eventually became self-aware. The Library is merely a physical manifestation of the thoughts and memories that make the Cursebearer. Our curse was not an act of malice, but a side-effect of our Elders coming into contact with a being of The Void."

Amalia's brow furrowed as she absorbed this information.

"If that is so, what happened to those who were cursed before us? And why did our Pact succeed in saving us and not them?"

Alaric crossed his arms over his chest.

"I could not know for sure without delving deeper than our Pact would allow. However, if I had to hazard a guess, it is likely that the King and Queen of The Fey simply extended the protection that their own realm has to us. It probably did not work for Elder Olbrecht and Elder Cennia, or the oldest of their children, because the damage that the touch of The Void had done was already too great. The King and Queen could grant us protection, but could not heal us from the damage that was already caused. As for what happens after that, the Cursebearer told me that when someone touched by The Void passes on, their memories and feelings are imprinted on him."

Amalia looked at Alaric with an unreadable look.

"That is why I chose to believe what the Cursebearer told me. He said he was instructed to speak with me, but his memories from the Elders also urged him to help."

Amalia shuffled in her chair again.

"Who would have instructed the Cursebearer to speak to you?"

Alaric shook his head.

"I do not know. Even the Cursebearer seemed concerned by being unable to know. He said that individual is in our world now, keeping watch for something. He said we would meet, and that I would know him when I saw him, but did not say much beyond that or when we would meet."

Amalia frowned.

"And with our lifespans that could mean hours or centuries."

Alaric nodded.

"Indeed. However, it is what this individual wanted the Cursebearer to tell me that concerned me. It is the true reason why I wished to speak with you immediately."

Amalia's frown turned into an unhappy scowl.

"What did he tell you?"

Alaric unfolded his arms and sat up straighter.

"He gave me a warning. The protection around our own world is currently very thin. The Void will try to take advantage of this and attempt to break into our world so it can devour it. It cannot act on its own, so it will attempt to have people in our world help it break through. The one who sent the warning wanted us to be vigilant, and not allow those people to act. We vampires have grown quite widespread in recent years. I thought it important that you were made aware of what the danger could be. I will leave it up to you whether or not you wish to make any other Elders aware of it."

Amalia looked down at the floor, clearly unhappy with this new responsibility.

"What do you think we should do?"

Alaric sat silently for several moments.

"I don't know. This is something that affects people far beyond just ourselves. I, myself, am unsure how best to decide. I was planning on calling all seven Aces together to discuss it with them. They too are individuals who, I believe, should be made aware of this. Their influence, especially Master Orpheus and Master Shepherd, will also allow us to better watch out for those who may be trying to cause our world harm."

Amalia pulled her feet up onto her chair and hugged her knees.

"So much is happening, in so little time. It feels overwhelming."

Alaric smiled gently and stood, walking over to Amalia. She looked up at him with a questioning look.

"There was one more message I was meant to pass along. One specifically for you, Amalia."

Amalia's eyebrows rose slightly.

Alaric reached out and carefully placed his hand on her head, her brow now furrowing in concern.

"Before the Cursebearer sent me back, he told me that Elder Olbrecht had something he wanted me to tell his child."

Amalia's breath caught.

"He wanted me to tell you that he is proud of you. Proud of how hard you have worked to protect everyone."

Tears welled up in Amalia's eyes and she buried her head against her knees and curled tightly into a ball.

Alaric smiled knowingly and made his way over to the door. He paused, his hand on the door handle, and looked over his shoulder.

"Good day to you, Amalia. May sleep bring you rest."

Alaric opened the door and slipped out of the room, closing the door behind him. He took a few moments to think and then headed down a passageway that led deeper into the Hive. His thoughts swam slowly through his tired mind and he tried, as well as he was able, to keep them where he needed them to be.

He approached a door and opened it slightly, knocking gently as he did.

"Can it wait? It's getting late and I was about to seek my bed."

Alaric grinned.

"My apologies, Master Faust, I needed to speak with you for a moment. Then we may both seek our beds."

Alaric saw Master Faust peek out from behind a machine at one end of the lab.

"Oh, young Alaric. Come in, my boy. It has been a hectic night, so I have only just placed the sample under the electron microscope. We will have the images in the evening."

Alaric chuckled.

"That's quite alright, Master Faust. I am in no real hurry to see the results of your testing. I actually came to bring you a message."

Master Faust shrugged and began untying his apron.

"Alright then, who decided you were the best one to be a message boy?"

"Elder Cennia."

Master Faust froze, the laces from his apron hanging limply in his hands.

"How is it that you have a message from my Mother?"

Alaric motioned to Master Faust.

"Perhaps it would be easiest if we spoke in your room. It is a long story."

Master Faust looked Alaric up and down several times before finally pulling off his apron.

"I imagine that it is, my boy. I imagine that it is."

16

Chapter Sixteen

Alaric spared a moment to glance up at the night sky, watching the stars twinkle in the clear early morning. After a while, he shook himself and headed into the Hive.

He made his way through the halls, winding back and forth through the mountain, and eventually found the door to his own room.

He quietly opened the door and stepped inside.

"Welcome back, My Love." Angelica called from a soft chair nearby, setting aside a book she had been reading and standing up to greet him.

Alaric smiled at her and let her kiss him and put her arms around him.

"I am back." He said quietly.

"Did you complete everything you needed to?" Angelica asked, stepping back after hugging him.

Alaric nodded.

"Yes, we were able to forge a complete set of seals. We should hopefully never need to be concerned with someone trying to gain access to The Library again."

Angelica smiled brightly.

"Does that mean we will be returning home then?"

Alaric laughed, taking one of Angelica's hands and raising it to his lips.

"Almost." He said, kissing the back of her hand. "In a few days."

Angelica frowned, pulling his hand to her mouth, and started biting the knuckles on his thumb.

"There is still more? I have nothing left to do, and I am growing bored."

Alaric grinned at her.

"I am sorry. There are just a few things left for me to finish." He paused, letting her gnaw on him for a few more moments. "Come with me to speak with Elder Amalia. I want to properly introduce you to Master Takanashi."

Angelica paused, looking up at Alaric.

"How many exaggerations have you told him about me?"

Alaric laughed, opening the door again and tugging gently on her hand.

"None at all."

Angelica frowned and gave him one more bite before following him out of the room.

"I don't think I believe you at all."

Alaric smiled and led the way, still holding Angelica's hand. They walked through the halls leading to the Elder's rooms, occasionally stepping aside to allow a guard to pass them with a bow.

As they approached Amalia's room, they saw that there were two guards posted outside.

"Is Elder Amalia available?" Alaric asked as they approached.

One of the guards nodded.

"Of course. They have been waiting for your arrival, Lord Alaric. The Elder also stated that she will permit Lord Angelica to enter as well."

Alaric nodded.

"Thank you. Continue the good work."

The guards bowed and Alaric stepped past, opening the door and allowing Angelica to walk through ahead of him.

Alaric followed Angelica inside and found that the room had been rearranged since the previous morning.

The plants and many of the small tables still lined the walls, but the chairs had been moved to the center of the main room. One of the coffee tables had been placed between the chairs, and a love seat had been brought in from somewhere else and placed at one end of the table.

Alaric could see that Mihail was sitting on one side of the table, and Master Ahanna and Master Takanashi were on the other side. Amalia sat at the head of the table, on the edge of her large armchair, her feet hanging just off the floor.

"I am glad you are here, Alaric. Thank you for coming. I am sure you would prefer to seek out your bed after everything you did today."

Alaric smiled politely at Amalia.

"I am happy to meet with everyone. I can find sleep after we are through with our discussion."

Alaric led Angelica around the love seat and motioned to her.

"Master Takanashi, I would like to introduce you to my Bloodbonded. This is Angelica."

Master Takanashi stood from his chair and bowed to Angelica. He was an older man, not very tall, with a head of nearly entirely gray hair.

"It is an honor to finally meet you, Angelica-Sama. Master Alaric speaks very fondly of you." Master Takanashi's accent was heavy, but his English still was very clear.

Angelica bowed in return, sparing Alaric a glance.

"I am sure whatever he told you was an exaggeration of the highest order. But, it is an honor to meet you as well, Master Takanashi."

Master Takanashi straightened and grinned, revealing a missing front tooth in a mouth full of otherwise well taken care of teeth.

Angelica smiled in return, self-consciously trying not to show her sharp canines.

Master Takanashi sat back down in his chair and Alaric gently pulled Angelica over to the love seat and they both sat down as well.

"May I say, before anything else, we are eternally grateful to Master Ahanna and Master Takanashi for giving their time and talents to aid us." Amalia started.

Master Ahanna shook her head.

"It was nothing. This Library was a dangerous place and needed to be protected. We are also always happy to give our aid to Master Alaric. He has helped, and taught, all of us in the past. Any chance we have to return his kindness is most welcome."

Master Takanashi simply nodded his agreement.

Amalia gave Alaric an amused look.

"We extend our gratitude to you regardless. We would like to continue having good relations with you, if at all possible. Especially seeing as there may be future need of you. If there is anything you need, that we can provide, please do not hesitate to let us know. We have Hives in every part of the world, and we will do our best to provide you with our aid."

Master Takanashi nodded, but Master Ahanna tilted her head to one side.

"You think you will have need of us again? Is there more to this Library than we initially believed?"

Alaric shook his head.

"No, The Library itself should no longer be a concern. It is what I learned while within it that is cause for concern."

Master Takanashi turned to look at Alaric.

"This concern you have, is it of note to more than just this Hive of vampires?"

Alaric nodded.

"I was warned that the world at large has need for concern. I was planning on bringing this up with the other four as well. Especially Master Orpheus and Master Shepherd."

Mihail glanced at Amalia, who nodded. He turned to face Alaric as well.

"What did you learn, Lord Alaric? Lady Amalia stated you had something important to speak of, but she did not elaborate to me."

Alaric leaned forward and placed his elbows on his knees. He felt Angelica place a supportive hand on his back.

"The one we vampires know as the Origin Cursebearer is a creature spawned of The Void. He was directed, by one unknown, to warn me that the protective veil between us and The Void is currently very thin. He believes that The Void will attempt to gain access to our world through individuals already within our own world."

Mihail frowned deeply, and Master Ahanna and Master Takanashi exchanged a concerned glance.

"Individuals seeking to ally themselves with The Void is, indeed, alarming." Master Ahanna said, trying to quickly think through the implications. "Master Orpheus and Master Shepherd have the widest influence, so I agree that they should be made aware quickly if we are to be watching for these individuals."

"I may soon have opportunity to speak with Master Koyane himself as well." Takanashi added. "His connections reach even wider than Master Shepherd's and he is a wise man."

Alaric nodded.

"I agree. If he is willing to aid us in keeping watch, that would be most helpful."

"What can we do?" Mihail asked.

Alaric looked back and forth between Amalia and Mihail a few times.

"Elder Amalia asked this of me when I first told her. I have given it some thought, and I believe we can be helpful in watching for individuals who have touched The Void. Our own Curse is merely the effects of making contact with an entity of The Void. Any vampire that is near someone who has experienced something similar should be able to sense them."

Mihail looked to Amalia, who nodded.

"Very well. We will bring this matter before the council. We will decide on a course of action that will allow us to dispatch Lord class vampires to places where suspected individuals may be hiding."

"If that is your plan, then we will watch for anything that will help us direct you where to look." Master Ahanna offered.

Alaric carefully scratched his chin.

"It is likely that anyone attempting to pierce the protective barrier of our world will generate an effect not unlike that of Outer Magic."

Master Takanashi nodded his agreement.

"That would be logical. Outer Magic is often considered illegal because of the negative effects it has on our world. An individual might even try to concentrate a high density of Outer Magic in one place in an attempt to pierce the barrier."

Alaric nodded.

"Agreed. We could likely call upon law enforcement worldwide to report instances of Outer Magic. Even if they are personal matters, it will at least allow us to separate the normal uses of Outer Magic from the effects caused by The Void."

"Perhaps we should task Master Orpheus with that." Master Ahanna suggested. "I believe his adopted son recently joined a detective agency."

Alaric nodded again.

"Yes. I believe young Leonidas was planning on an apprenticeship with a detective near their branch of The Academy. Though, that was delayed some time ago due to an accident and I have been so busy of late that I have not had the time to ask Master Orpheus about it. When I return to the United States, I will appraise Master Orpheus and Master Shepherd of the situation and inquire as to the young man's recovery. Perhaps he will already know individuals who can make reports for us."

"Might I then suggest that all information, that we all receive, be collected by Alaric?" Amalia grinned when Alaric frowned. "Do not worry, I have good reason for suggesting as much."

Alaric sighed and leaned back. Angelica scooted closer to him and reached her arm around him.

"Very well. Why do you wish me to bear this responsibility, Elder?"

Amalia motioned with one hand, clearly starting to enjoy herself.

"You are the one who connects us all. That alone is reason enough, but there is more. I believe it is in our best interest to ensure that everything we collect be held in confidence. Of all our Hives, the Great Plains

Hive is the most secure. Even more so than the Elder Hive. I, of course, will not ask that you take on this work along with everything else you already do. I will involve Hivelord Andros, and we will act quickly to replace Overlord Burchard with two new Overlords. One to maintain the day-to-day work of the Hive, and one to aid you in all other work you need a hand with."

All eyes in the room turned to Alaric.

Alaric sighed.

"Very well, Elder. I cannot fault your logic."

Amalia clapped her hands together excitedly.

"Excellent. Then as a second order of business, Lord Angelica, I would like to offer you the position of Second Overlord of the Great Plains Hive. Working under the sole direction of Underlord Alaric."

Angelica blinked in surprise.

"Me? Are you certain, Elder? I am not really well suited for the work of an Overlord."

Amalia grinned happily.

"I am most certain. The regular day-to-day work of Overlord will be done by another of the Council's choosing. I need someone I know we can trust to serve specifically with Underlord Alaric to ensure the safety and security of the Hive. Also to aid Underlord Alaric in whatever duties he may have need." Amalia's grin widened. "I am afraid that would mean you would have to spend most of your waking hours with Underlord Alaric."

Angelica glanced sideways at Alaric, who was doing his best not to look anywhere but the floor.

"Well, if you believe I am worthy of the position, Elder." Angelica looked back at Amalia with a smile and bowed her head. "Then I will strive to perform my duties to the best of my ability."

"We will bring your acceptance before the Council." Mihail said. "Thank you, and congratulations to you, Overlord Angelica."

Angelica felt Alaric slide his arm around her.

"Are you sure you won't regret your decision? You have to take orders from me now."

Angelica leaned back and pinned Alaric's arm against the back of the love seat.

"As if I would listen to you any more or less than I do now." She looked over at Alaric, who now grinned at her, and she suddenly felt her cheeks growing warm.

"Then perhaps we shall take our leave." Master Takanashi said, standing up with a slight grumble. "Master Ahanna and I will be leaving shortly, and I am certain that you all will be wishing to find rest soon."

Amalia smiled and nodded politely as Master Ahanna stood as well.

"Thank you again for all you have done. Please keep Alaric appraised of all you learn, and feel free to visit us again in the future. You will be welcome here at anytime."

Master Ahanna bowed to Amalia.

"Thank you for your hospitality. It was an honor to meet you, and a privilege to work with you."

Master Ahanna walked over to Angelica and bowed, using both her hands to lift Angelica's free hand.

"It was also an honor to meet you, Angelica. I do hope we will have the opportunity to speak again. Perhaps you can gossip to me of Master Alaric next time, so that you may not feel as if he is the only one who can do so."

Angelica felt her cheeks start burning, but tried to smile.

"Thank you, Master Ahanna. I hope we can meet again as well." She turned her face away slightly. "I'm not sure I could bring myself to gossip though."

Alaric chuckled quietly.

"You never know, you might have fun if you try."

Angelica frowned at Alaric.

"Are you trying to get bitten?"

"Are you offering?" He asked her.

Angelica pouted, letting go of Master Ahanna's hands and trying to cover her face.

Master Ahanna smiled and bowed slightly to Alaric before following Master Takanashi out of the room.

Amalia hopped down from her chair and hurried over to Angelica, grabbing her hand and pulling it away from her face.

"I want to meet with you again too. Sometime when I am not needed by the Council. I would very much like you to try on more dresses with me. I must insist you visit me at my estate once again. Perhaps once the Elder Council is out of session?"

Angelica felt her cheeks grow even hotter but was mildly relieved when Alaric came to her rescue.

"I am afraid we will have to leave before then, Elder. I can spare a day or two to help Master Faust, but then we must return to the United States so that planning for the next full moon can begin."

Amalia pouted.

"I suppose I cannot reasonably ask that the full moon be delayed."

Alaric laughed.

"If we could, then I am sure the werewolves would have far less to be concerned about. Besides, we also have a great deal to do if we want to be prepared for all of the new work we will be receiving."

Amalia crossed her arms over her chest, still pouting.

"Perhaps I should not have suggested it."

Mihail stood from his chair, a slight smile touching one corner of his lips.

"The best we can do is find a new First Overlord for the Great Plains Hive and ensure that they have all the resources they will need. To be quite honest, the Great Plains Hive has grown very large and is overdue for a second overlord. It is only due to Lord Alaric's skill, and Hivelord Andros' foresight, that the Council has not felt the need to make a decision in the matter. Perhaps, if we act quickly, Lord Alaric and Lord Angelica may then have the time to visit again."

Amalia put one hand on her chin in thought.

"Perhaps I should ask for in-person quarterly reports from those involved."

"If we can avoid that, I will agree to find a time to return for a visit." Alaric said quickly, and Amalia grinned.

"Oh, well then, perhaps email reports might suffice instead."

Alaric smiled and stood, helping Angelica to her feet.

"Thank you, Elder. I think we will retire to our bed now as well."

Amalia pouted again but nodded and they both bowed to the two Elders before turning and leaving the room.

After walking down the hall for a moment, and when Angelica was certain no one was around to see, she slipped behind Alaric and jumped on his back.

Alaric paused a moment with a smile, then grabbed her legs and continued down the hall with her on his back.

"Are you truly so tired?" He asked.

He felt Angelica shake her head and then she started chewing on his shoulder.

"No, but I owe you some bites."

Epilogue

Angelica stood silently on a rooftop, looking out over the city. Everything was quiet, and the city was still. She took a deep breath through her nose, not sensing anything out of the ordinary.

She pulled her phone from her pocket and checked it. Everyone in her group was reporting all clear, and her last message from Alaric had stated that there were no incidents nearby.

Out of the corner of her eye, she noticed a movement. She turned her head and scanned the streets and alleys until she saw a man walking down the middle of one of the roads.

As soon as her eyes fell on him, the man froze. She watched in interest as he looked around for a few moments and was then surprised when his head swiveled and he looked directly back at her. She was even more surprised to see the man grin and then wave to her.

Her eyebrows furrowed, not certain what was happening, and then she leaped from one building to the next until she reached the street the man was on.

She dropped down and landed lightly on the ground next to the man. She straightened and pushed some hair out of her face.

"What kind of person thinks it is wise to walk around in the open on the night of a full moon?" She asked him, inspecting him more closely.

The man smiled politely at her.

"Perhaps a fool, I think. It is a pleasure to see you again, Lady Angelica."

Angelica tilted her head slightly, thinking the voice was familiar. Then she suddenly remembered a shattered apartment building from months before.

"Liam! I almost didn't recognize you. Must be because you don't look like you're about to have a panic attack."

Liam chuckled.

"Yeah, living at Koyane Manor has done me more good than years of therapy ever did."

Angelica grinned, subconsciously trying not to reveal her fangs.

"Glad to hear it. Alaric will be pleased to hear you are doing well. What are you doing out here though?"

Liam half turned and pointed at a white ribbon pinned to his shirt sleeve.

"I got permission to help patrol during the full moon. Since they started using traps to catch stray werewolves, I figured I could act as the perfect bait to lure them in."

Angelica frowned slightly.

"Are you sure that is wise?"

Liam laughed, a bit halfheartedly.

"Still makes me a bit nervous, but thanks to Mistress Olivia and Master Shepherd I am a lot faster than I used to be. I am pretty confident now in my ability to outrun a werewolf."

Angelica put her hands on her hips and shook her head.

"Never imagined I would see you change so dramatically in such a short time."

Liam grinned.

"I met with Master Shepherd and he sat down with me and talked through what it meant to carry an Aspect. It was like all the jumbled-up pieces of my entire life just suddenly," He lifted his arms and swept his hands out in front of him. "fell into place."

Angelica smiled back.

"That is good. I'm happy to hear we were able to help you find your home."

She felt her phone vibrate and pulled it from her pocket. She looked over it with a frown.

"Well, it was a nice chat, but it looks like there could be a Waif prowling around on the north side."

Liam held up one hand.

"There is a trap set up over there. Let me respond to this one. It was nice to talk to you again. I hope the rest of your night is peaceful."

Liam turned and raced off with the speed of an Olympic sprinter. He didn't look like he would even break a sweat as he disappeared down the street.

Angelica shook her head, turning back towards the buildings.

"Kid really is quick on his feet."

The End

www.ingramcontent.com/pod-product-compliance
Lightning Source LLC
Chambersburg PA
CBHW070953180726
48291CB00004B/1279